D1327340

ACHILLES

Elizabeth Cook's poetry and short stories have appeared in *Agenda, Tears in the Fence, Kunapipi* and *The Penguin Book of Erotic Stories by Women.* She is the author of *Seeing Through Words* (Yale University Press) and the editor of *John Keats* (Oxford University Press), *The Alchemist* by Ben Jonson and *The Roaring Girl* by Middleton and Dekker (both A&C Black).

ACHILLES
Elizabeth Cook

Methuen

10 9 8 7 6 5 4 3 2 1

First published in Great Britain in 2001 by Methuen Publishing Ltd
215 Vauxhall Bridge Rd, London SW1V 1EJ

Copyright © 2001 by Elizabeth Cook
The right of Elizabeth Cook to be identified as the author
of this work has been asserted by her in accordance with
the Copyright, Designs and Patents Act 1988

Methuen Publishing Limited Reg. No. 3543167

A CIP catalogue record for this book
is available from the British Library

ISBN 0 413 75740 4

Designed by Bryony Newhouse

Printed and bound in Great Britain by
St Edmundsbury Press Limited, Bury St Edmunds, Suffolk

for Jonathan Nevitt

I am very grateful to Greg Hicks. This work might not have been completed without his enthusiasm for it in its early stages and his readiness to voice what had been written and embody it in performance.

Contents

TWO RIVERS

Two Rivers

Two rivers. Flowing in contrary directions.

Two layers of water, each moving steadily, separate and self-possessed.

It is as if membrane divides them.

The upper flow, when the sun catches it, is sharp green. Chlorophyll: essence of life. Life teems in this water, gives it its green. Even from a boat you can see the fish streaming through, swift, thick as a rain of arrows. It doesn't take much to skim some off for a meal which lingers in the smoky, charred bits of flesh and skin that stick to your fingers till you rake at the bits and gnaw them off with your teeth to suck up the last of the salt.

The other river, which seems to run sluggish against the grain of the swift-flowing, sparkling green, attempting to turn it? What colour is this? Is it no colour? Would it have colour if the sun gashed it? Yes. Then it is sapphire blue; but mostly it appears black.

Nothing lives in this water. It is anoxic: hostile to life.

There is a passage of sea where these waters rope together to form a single cable. This cable has carried Odysseus to the edge of Ocean. There was no gainsaying its pull. Hand over fist it dragged the boat on till all at once they reached the place where the waters untwist and drop their cargo. Again the rivers assert their separateness. Only now it is the black that is uppermost. It seems to go on for ever and there is no movement in it. Nothing helps or hinders Odysseus and his men as they row to the shore – a shore not lapped by sea. The water just lies there, pooled like a lake. There is no breath but their own.

When they step into it, it is as warm as their own blood. So is the air. The exact heat of blood; not a jot hotter or colder. It is dark as an oven. Thick cloud covers the stars (if there are stars and it is night – the men have lost track) and with no sensation of temperature to define them it is hard to know where their bodies begin and end. Some of them slap and rub their hands over themselves for reassurance.

Another island. Another stop on the journey home.

Circe told Odysseus to come here, to follow the stream of Ocean till he came to the mouth of Hell; to the rock where two tributaries of Styx meet Acheron. Her instructions were detailed:

Dig a pit a cubit deep, a cubit wide each way, and fill this tank with drink that will satisfy the dead.

Milk, honey, wine, water.

All this is sprinkled with barley which bobs on the surface like scum. Odysseus prays; makes promises to the dead. Tells them what he will do for them when he gets home. *When* he gets home!

A ram and a black ewe have travelled with them from Circe's island, bleating tirelessly all the way but most protestingly just now, being dragged through the tight wood to the clearing.

First, the ewe.

Short close hair. Odysseus grasps the folds of flesh above the neck and tugs back her head. The point of his blade is exact. Blood pours from the creature's throat in a generous arc. The ram rears and bucks. One of Odysseus' men has to straddle him to hold him down while his throat too is cut. His blood drums into the drink pit like horse piss where it foams and steams.

Ah! That's more like it.

Milk and honey, wine and barley are all very well. They are right and proper. They are due. But they are not what the dead want. Now that the blood is soaking into the earth tank, making a rich mud of the floor, the flavour trickles down into Hades.

They arrive suddenly. So many of them, jostling and pushing – elbows, knees, necks – forcing their way forward, their mouths leading. Their mouths aflame.

Only at the very beginning did the living outnumber the dead. Now, as the dead press forward, Odysseus has great difficulty in standing his ground. Circe had told him what would happen. But not *what it would be like.*

The sound of them. The sound of dis-satisfaction.

Of layer upon layer of longing.

Achilles senses Odysseus long before he sees him. He has come up to the mouth of Hell with the others. To his great displeasure he has no choice. He would like to have stayed where he was, in Pluto's rich labyrinth, remembering life, knowing it in words. He can still speak better than all the rest, now, when he can no longer act and make a difference

– not even dent the waters he bathes in. But the smell of the blood in that tank cannot be resisted. The flavour of iron seeps through the earth and the rocks, reaching Achilles and all the other dead. The fine veins that riddle the rocks are filled with it; the rocks themselves are suffused. The longing hooks into his heart and pulls him.

It is intolerable. He, who has always lived by his own necessity, who had choices and made them. To be dragged, helpless as a fish.

You would not think him helpless to look at him. He stands apart with Patroclus, his beloved through all eternity, and Patroclus – who loves Achilles but not so much as he is loved – waits for Achilles to move. His deference to Achilles is different from that of the others. They honour and respect him, keep a wise distance, because Achilles was better than all the rest. Better at being human. Fighting, singing, speaking, raging (oh, he is good at that still). Killing. But Patroclus alone is humbled by Achilles' love. Only a fool thinks that to be more loved than loving gives power. Only a fool vaunts it and displays his own littleness by bragging to his friends and making capricious demands of his lover. Patroclus isn't a fool. He knows that he is less than Achilles even in this. Humbled by the immensity of Achilles' love he loves him back with all his large, though lesser, heart.

The two remain silent, in control of themselves, while the other shades cram themselves in to whatever space they can find near the blood-tank. Like dogs they are; tongues hanging out, oblivious to all but their thirst and whatever blocks their way. Achilles cannot see what it is. Is that

Tiresias' voice? The pitch of the man-woman; not a chord but a harmonic in which treble and bass combine and are distinct. Only Tiresias whacks out the words in that insistant, circling rhythm, like a whirlwind whipping through trees in a grove, circling and beating, then suddenly still. Then off again.

But Achilles cannot make out what the words are.

Then women's voices. He sees them: tall, graceful, slender as saplings. Aristocrats among women, wives and daughters of princes, lovers of gods. Each of them, bent with longing for a sup of that steaming blood. He can't make out all of them – many are cowled – but he catches sight of Phaedra, wiping her red-smudged mouth with her forearm, blinking from light.

Is Iphigeneia here? Perhaps she can resist.

She entered the underworld fearlessly, heart open, undeviating as one of his arrows; the way she pushed up through the wind, up the hill to Artemis' shrine.

That was the first time Agamemnon tried to make a fool of him: fetching him in to be her husband. To Agamemnon a ruse – 'Tell her she's going to be married to Achilles.' That would get Clytemnestra excited; get her cooperating, full of maternal pride and vicarious lust. Agamemnon had no sense then – or ever – of how well-matched Achilles and Iphigeneia really were. In spite of Agamemnon Achilles had greeted her clean heart. She decided, not her father – not even the gods – that she belonged to Artemis. She showed him that the way to make your fate your choice is to choose it, fearlessly, your lungs drinking the air. It makes the gods ashamed.

Here in the underworld she has not gone stale. A glimpse

of her and you feel you have brushed your sight against new leaves. A sense of green, where there is none.

This is what happens when you are dead:

You know the living are up there, driving your horses, ploughing your fields, handling your bowls. Eating. The living are always eating; their tongues fossicking among the bones.

They make use of your cloths. Your armour. You sense them, hear their footfalls; almost you can see them. In your mind it is clearer than when you were there but your eyes have lost the power to focus on matter. You can't hear them properly. The words they speak, real as bread when you spoke among them, are muffled like the words of foreign tribes. You don't know their edges.

The shade of Agamemnon pushes past. A bit too eager. Rein yourself in you greedy fool. You always liked blood that was shed at no risk to yourself. Still hiding behind your title of King. Everything you had was on account of that. Nothing was earned by your nature. You never saw any of it but the having. The Achaean warriors (who showed their greatness, not yours, in giving you loyalty) you made your instruments. Even Cassandra to you was just a cunt – a royal one – on legs. Every time you missed the point because the point you wanted to make was 'Agamemnon is glorious.' Easy then for your wife to trick you. Red carpets. A bath like a cauldron. All that mocking pomp. She was another one you never saw. Not even when her knife went in and your own blood pumped unstoppably into the bath. Down here it is still 'Agamemnon is glorious' but now your other chant is 'Women are treacherous.' You never stopped to think why Clytemnestra wished you dead.

Achilles hears the drone of Agamemnon's voice. Even in the underworld he finds an audience. Now he's talking with one of the living. Still trying to impose his little will up there.

Achilles can't make out what he's saying. Not that he cares.

There are tears in Agamemnon's eyes as he moves back into the dark. He flinches from Achilles' gaze. Achilles glimpses Agamemnon as a man, shortlived and ignorant.

The way is clear now. The pit is at his feet.

He doesn't muzzle his way in like the others but kneels beside the pit as if it were a pool of clear rock water. Graceful as a nymph he dips a hand in and drinks from it; dips again and offers it to Patroclus, who drinks.

Sight clears.

Odysseus.

Who else?

'So you're still there.'

Reproach or admiration? Odysseus is not sure. Or does Achilles mock him? He has always made him feel that he tries too hard.

Achilles does laugh – from pleasure at seeing his old companion, stocky and foursquare and stinking with life.

'Odysseus, son of Laertes, now I know you'll stop at nothing. Is no adventure too exacting or repugnant for you? For you it's the harder the better: the more nearly impossible the greater you show. And you've still got some companions left.'

Achilles stares back through the night. He can just make out Odysseus' men where they crowd round the fire: see a cheek, a hand in the light of the flame; they are turned away, not seeing the shades that Odysseus sees and speaks with. What Achilles would give to stand around that fire with them, to warm his hands, stir up the cinders with an old sword's point. And then to hunker down and eat.

But now, another hunger.

'What's the news of my father? He's old now. How does he manage without me to defend him? Do the Myrmidons respect him? Honour him? Does he keep his land – the land I should be farming? How did he take my death?'

He knows that nothing – not earfuls of prophecy – can prepare a father for the death of his son. It is an offence which nothing can ever make good.

'And my son, Neoptolemus. Where is he? How did he fight at the end of the war? Is he safe? Tell me, Odysseus. No one here knows anything.'

Odysseus shakes his head. He has come to this border-land to question Tiresias; to learn how, if ever, he will reach his own father and home in Ithaka again. He wants to know. And this is what the dead want too. Every one of them – queens, princesses, kings of men – has asked for news. They have forgotten how hard it is for the living to know things. That the rule is one place at one time. The way they claw at him – it's as if they expect him to have been everywhere at once. The truth is he's as ignorant as they were. As they still are.

'Noble Achilles, son of Peleus, you see what condition you find me in. Hardships come upon me like walled waters, keeping me from home, from my own father, my son, my wife. My companions fall off one by one, tumble into the sheer-sided pit. Those years we camped on the plain by Troy were nothing in their hardship to what I have endured since that city fell. I have no news of your father Peleus. He must still walk the earth or he'd be here; but in what condition I cannot say. But I do know about Neoptolemus.'

Odysseus stays Achilles. At last he has something to give this terrible, hungry man. It was he, Odysseus, who extracted Neoptolemus from the court at Skiros and carried him over the sea in his beaked ship to the other Achaeans camped on the plain. He heard the boy word-spar with Nestor, saw the old man's eyes gleam like an old, experienced wrestler's when he finds a pupil who can rouse him. Odysseus can tell Achilles how his son was the first to climb out of the hollow horse:

'He fought on till Priam's palace had no life left in it, not Priam's, not any kin of his. His skill, his courage, his power unextinguishable.

'All harm came from him. No harm came to him.'

Achilles is proud for his son. He hopes it will be many years before they meet at last down here.

But for himself there is no point in pride. Odysseus, the reputation-seeker, envies Achilles.

'We honoured you like a god while you were alive. No one could match you. Now that you're dead we still speak of you as one who will never be surpassed. Here too I see you're a king.'

A mistake. A moment ago Achilles had needed Odysseus. Now he lets him go, his face dark with scorn.

'What's that to me? Don't you know that it's sweeter to be *alive* – in any shape or form – than lord of all these shadows?'

He strides away, leaving Odysseus unblessed.

Quicken

But first, a quickening:

A mortal gets to do what the king of the gods is afraid of.

How *do* you mate with Thetis, the sea-nymph that the gods desire?

'The main thing,' says Chiron, 'is not to let go.'

He too would like to pin her under his hooves.

What would it be like?

'She will do everything she can to throw you – buck, kick, bite, *dissolve*, shrink and grow thorns. You like them lively? This one is flame of life itself. If you want her – and you must, Zeus requires it – you have to hold fast, even to flame.

'You'll be burnt, and it will be worth it.'

Peleus is a patient man. He can spend three days listening to petitions, hearing each man have his say, judging the merits of each case, without any sign of irritation or weariness. Each man who comes to him feels he's the first: that this beautiful, vigorous king wants to be nowhere else on earth but here, seated and attentive.

He is patient in hunting too. Even as a boy, before he had strength – just the courage that builds it – he was able to wait. He knew that the best meat is the meat of an animal who has died without fear. Fear poisons meat, clogs the fibres. The hunter who puts fear in his prey will end up feeding on it.

So he stalks her.

Thetis the sea-nymph, allocated to him by Zeus who wanted her himself but didn't dare to lay a godly finger on her because of what the son she'd bear him would do to him.

No one has bothered to ask Thetis if this *man* they have chosen for her will do. No one has shown her one good reason why she should let some mortal enter her.

So he stalks her.

She, on her own, is perfectly happy, unpenetrated by man or god. The sea and the air make love to her daily, know each fold and whorl of her, every line of foot and hand, every cleft and dimple. She comes from the sea and is made of it, but separate in her woman's shape she can enjoy it more, dive cleanly into it, ride on it, play. Sometimes she turns herself into a wheel and rolls round and round on herself in the water; then she straightens out to move like an arrow down to the sea bed where she grazes the floor along with the flat-bellied fish. When she comes out she lies slabbed on a rock while the sun licks her dry.

The last thing she wants is some man clambering all over her.

So he stalks her.

She has come to this place for eight days now. A little bay, shaped like a new moon, cradling the sea between the delicate horns of its headlands. The sand on the beach is shockingly white: if a crab moves across, denting the drift with heavy claw, its darkness can be seen from the cliffs above. You don't need eagle eyes to see like an eagle here, everything is so sharpened and magnified. Beyond the beach, some rocks. Vegetation. A cave, sandy-floored, cool, its entrance screened by myrtle.

A good lookout.

Only Thetis does not look out. She sleeps, confident that only birds and animals know this place.

While she sleeps Peleus watches her, the myrtle his screen too. She is lying on her back, left arm stretched up, face turned towards it. Her right knee slightly bent.

What would it take to take her?

He watches her all afternoon. The sun, all stealth, slides in and lays itself along her like a sword. She does not wake and the sun moves on.

Peleus waits and watches; getting to know the shape of her, the edges of bone and the warm furrows. The heft of her as he'll lift her on his cock.

Feet quiet, close as dust, all edges but one softened.

Now!

So little violence required: just enough to clasp her waist with two hands, tip her back into an arch, hold her steady while he scabbards himself fast.

Now!

His right arm scooped under her back, knee wedging thighs apart. She wakes to the man covering her, darkening her like a tent, coming between her and the light.

Her arched back held, she arches more

and bucks.

Her body now one sentient muscle:

A HEART,

AN EEL,

A FISH.

He feels the charge of her bucking like a thunderbolt. It flings him breathless to the ground.

On his back now.

Hold on!

As he falls he reaches out, pulls on whatever substance his fingers find. It burns him and his fingers stick. If he were to pull away his skin would come away too, charred like fish-skin stuck to hot stone.

Has he become fish to meet her?

But she is fire now. Roped flame. A long exhalation of searing heat. Tongue upon tongue of it, each twined on itself, an avid, wildly flickering spiral. Howling with pain he opens his throat and drinks in the flame. He'll be *her* scabbard, her sheath, her cup. No lover entered him so thoroughly.

But she is not yet lover.

He tries to hold on; to cleave to the flame that cores him, to move in closer, tighter.

Not rope but thread now.

A fine fuse.

Close now. Move with it. Let it tune you. Notice how it gets sharper as it gets finer: that should help you stay with it.

Whatever you do, hold on; keep it in view.

But Peleus, cored by this flame, is dissolving. The rest of him is falling away. What is there in him that can follow?

There is nothing of him to hold on with.

Not fire now, but water.

Does she think to elude him? She cools him. Restores him to his edge. Rinses his scalded, crazy flesh so it feels clear again.

But as she streams off him she starts to flee – as water – into the sand.

DON'T LEAVE ME!

He sprawls across the ground, crushing himself into it. He takes up damp sand in fistfuls and plasters it across his chest. She'll not get away. He'll have her, *he'll find her*, whatever form she takes to.

Even a lion's?

Even a lion's.

A lion now, she straddles him; would maul him between her huge paws but he wraps himself round her, legs and arms clasping her trunk as she tries, at this awkward angle, to take his head into the cave of her mouth. She can't reach and his wrap around her tightens. The lion Thetis feels herself squeezed almost beyond bearing. Held now, she wants not so much to escape as to fight. Being squeezed she lets herself go beyond the point where breath is lost – where lion expires – brings herself smaller, tighter, so she is now one lithe tube.

A snake.

So narrow she could slip away if she chose.

She's coiled herself around him and now it is he who is near to expiring for want of breath. For a moment he panics. He is near to losing all the benefit of Chiron's wisdom, about to go against the will of Zeus and Juno, and let go.

Only he can't. She has him so fast in her grip. Now her snake tongue darts into his mouth and its sharpness is so sweet to him he wants to hold it there. Practised on the filament of fire he concentrates the whole of his being on drawing that sweet sting out of her.

So they ride for a while, she fast around his body, covering him with her coils; he fast around the fine pulse of her tongue, intent on extracting its bag of nectar.

He feels it will happen soon. She is gathering herself. The tongue is withdrawn. He is still held fast but the dryness of snakeskin has gone; replaced by flesh which is softer, wetter. More enveloping.

Ten pulsing arms are lapping him and on their undersides are a great many mouths which adhere to him: tiny, searching mouths suckling on him; rubbing his flesh against the bony ridge of their toothless gums. There is no surface of his body that she – this cuttlefish – does not contact and which he in turn does not long to have drawn up and used by her. He is very near to losing himself – and if he does so he'll lose her, though just now he doesn't have the mind to care.

Now she has stopped escaping him. She needs him to find her. She cannot feel beyond the next need which is that the nub, the palate of each tiny mouth, be met by him; pursued right in to the tight star which burns at its centre.

He has no choice. The labyrinth now has no false corridors. He can only travel to the centre.

Hit.

Met.

The stars dissolve.

He is covered in sticky black ink.

Thetis, a woman, under him. He draws himself up for a moment to look on his new wife with tenderness. Then he turns her over, enters her again, and empties himself of all the forms he has been.

Neither of them wake until the sun has removed itself from the beach.

～

ACHILLES IS the seventh.

Six times Thetis has taken a wet new infant up by the heels and dunked it, umbilicus trailing, in the Styx where she'd let it go.

'Immortality,' she said, 'I'm burning away their mortal parts in the fire of this river.'

'You're drowning my sons,' he said.

'They're living on Olympus,' she said.

'Not with me they're not,' he said.

The next time they made love he became an eagle (he'd learnt) and in the after-sleep he dreamed of holding his son in his beak and flying him free of scalding waters. When the seventh son comes she begins again on the same rigmarole, but she lingers over it more, holding him by the left ankle as she turns him in the fiery waters, basting him on every side.

The burning baby yells with all the force of unimpeded lungs. Peleus comes running – that sound has hooked into his bowels – and wrenches the child from her grasp. Just a little patch of flesh unburnt: the area held between pincers of thumb and forefinger.

For weeks, using all the skill that Chiron has given him, he tends the poor burnt flesh of his child.

Till Achilles is as mortal as he.

His Girlhood

The world is never large enough to hide in.

Thetis has always known the war would come; that any son of hers would be moth to its flames. What she can do she does. She trains him in the arts of being a girl and takes him – her lovely daughter Pyrrha – to the court of King Lycomedes at Skiros...

       where she tips him

                      into the shoal of girls.

... watched by Deidamia, King Lycomedes' daughter.

When Deidamia catches a fish, she keeps it in a bowl for a while, watches it curvet and turn, imagines she is training it as her father trains his horses. Then she'll tip the fish back into the water it came from, follow it with her eyes... till with one quick turn the fish dissolves the trail and she can no longer tell it from all the rest.

This fish – the one that Thetis slides into the shoal – goes on being different. Deidamia, half-concealed by a pillar, observes the strange new girl:

Auburn hair in tight coils down to the collar bone; long

limbs; a straight and supple back. This Pyrrha does not smile as the other girls would have done. She appears not to mind whether anyone likes her.

Deidamia wants this fish for herself.

Achilles knows perfectly well that the girl is watching him. Not just this one; all of them. It is new, this sensation of being stared at from all sides. It's like standing in the sun at midday, feeling the heat cooking you. Only in sunlight you can strut or box the air, make little eddies in the heat. These twenty-five pairs of girls' eyes on him make him less free to move. He wishes he were busy at something – whittling some wood to a spear point would be good – but his mother took his knife from him when she dressed him in this thin girl's tunic. He fiddles with the bracelets on his arm; turns them, draws them up to the wrist and lets them fall back towards his elbow. The gentle clash of metal.

With these eyes still on him he burns. Senses his power.

These are the bodies Achilles knows:

1. Thetis'. Made of the sea. Cool hands that refresh him; wash pain away; wash away blood and dirt from his limbs. Her silent gowns are greens and blues and silver grey. This body is there whenever he seeks it but he does not caress it or know its contours – just the feel of it rinsing heat away.

2. Chiron's body. Wide horse back to straddle, vault and sometimes arc yourself across. Man's waist, chest and

shoulders rising firm, sure as a prow. So many textures
and smells in one body: close nap of horse hair, darker
along the spine and set at a different angle; the sticky,
resinous feel of this pelt if you run your hand against
the grain; the silky, hairless flesh near the genitals – a
place of comfort and burrowing. A hoof, knocking his
cheek in reproof when he tries, exploring, to prise out
the pouched, retracted member. The smells of man
sweat and horse sweat; the mat of springy blonde curls
on chest and beard that he'd tugged as a baby, still tugs
sometimes now. This body taught him itself and nearly
all else. The hoof that drew shapes in the dust showed
him how stars moved.

3. His father's body: less intimately known than Chiron's
but also loved and familiar. A stillness in Peleus like
rock. Watching him sometimes you'd wonder if he'd
ever move again. Then when he does move it is swift as
a snake's tongue. A body smoother than Chiron's – you
can trace where the flesh puckers and coarsens into
scar. Each wound a story. When he was small Achilles
would choose a scar and poke it with his finger,
demanding a tale which ended *here*; testing to see if the
story was the same as the last time. In his mind he cast
a net over Peleus' body. Where the lines joined there
were scars. He learned how to spin a story from link to
link, from scar to scar. These, the stories of his father's
body, were his first.

He also knows the body of his cousin Patroclus.

But the nearest he has got to a girl's body is his own, togged up like this.

Deidamia plays host. She goes up to Pyrrha and takes both hands as if to tug her into the circle of a game.

'Come. I'll show you my favourite place.'

She leads Pyrrha out of the palace, past her father's stables to where there is open plain. Then she drops Pyrrha's hand and runs and Achilles – though he has to hold himself back so as not to overtake her – does not have to go as slowly as Thetis had told him to. They run to where the plain stops and woodland begins. Deidamia knows a path and leads her new friend through a maze of trees till the soft ground changes to rock. As the trees thin out you hear water. High slabbed boulders jut over a river in spate. Deidamia scrambles up the highest boulder and waves down to Pyrrha who follows.

'Look how the water pounces on that rock. And there, where it sucks itself into a tunnel.'

Achilles breaks off a segment of pine cone and aims it at the funnel of water; they take it in turns to drop things in – a leaf, a twig, a berry – see how the water catches them.

'Let's swim,' says Deidamia.

Achilles, suddenly bashful, hangs back while the princess races ahead to a clearing where the sun burns hot through the trees and smooth rocks frame a deep, hardly-moving pool. Where the river takes a breath.

As soon as she gets there she drags her shift off. The gesture is nothing like the one he's learnt girls use. He has never seen a naked girl before – the little puffs of breasts, the rounded stomach. It looks so soft compared with his.

Like him she has some new silky hairs below her belly but no penis juts out of them. He feels for his prick through the cloth of his girl's tunic. Pats it to reassure himself; does something else entirely.

Deidamia is now bobbing around in the water.

'Jump in Pyrrha. Can't you swim?'

Feeling stupid, trying to hold his tunic down across his thighs, Achilles slithers down between the cleft of two rocks; joins her in the heavenly cool water. Deidamia embraces him – or rather Pyrrha – with cold, fresh-watery kisses. She dives down and sees – in spite of his efforts – what he's been attempting to hide. She comes up laughing and kisses him again. They find the inside of each other's lips – smooth and hot and very unlike the water they bob in and keep swallowing as they struggle to keep afloat. Only when they have pulled themselves out of the water does Achilles take off his dress and spread it out across a wide flat rock to dry.

Later that day, when they have arrived back at the court, Deidamia announces to her friends that Pyrrha will be sharing her bed. Does Lycomedes know of these arrangements? He says nothing.

They often go out to the bathing pool. The other girls respect their friendship. At court Pyrrha is thought quiet and modest. A better musician than any of them, but she will not sing; a tireless dancer; good at all their games.

For Achilles these days of girlhood complete the education Chiron began. Refine it; soften his burning impatience.

He learns to listen, dawdle, play. Delighting in Deidamia he becomes adept as Pyrrha. He borrows Deidamia's dresses, wanting to feel how her body feels – not just to his hands but to herself – when her soft silks drift over it. He uses her sweetest oils on his skin and hair, lets her plait flowers into his curls.

But there are times when girlhood chafes and his underused limbs ache to be stretched. Then he slips off; takes another path into the woods to a cave he's found, removes his girl clothes and bracelets, binds his hands with strips of cloth and starts to box. He jabs the air, mapping its emptiness into a thousand precise locations. *Forward – over a little – now yield to the right. Cover. Cover. Now punch and get out.*

He hears Chiron's commentary in his mind, urging him on. He makes a bag of a piece of hide, fills it with stones and suspends it from a tree. He uses this to test his hands and feet against.

He longs to be met. To find an opponent who will answer each move with countermove; who will weigh him up and see him. Daily as he trains he dreams of this opponent. Builds him in thought.

He finds a tall pine to climb from where he can look out over the island and across the sea. The number of ships is growing. In a hollowed-out tree nearby some bees have built a nest. He speaks to them, observes how they organise themselves. Steals their honey for Deidamia.

From his pine tree lookout he sees the ship with the rust-coloured sails. It is still a long way off but he senses it is aiming at him. He feels the circle tightening.

The air in the court alters when the three men arrive. Odysseus: stocky, legs a bit too short for his body. A sense of compressed power. Ajax like a god. Huge. Well-made – looks like he could eat you and three oxen for breakfast. Then Nestor: older than the other two, more contained, his face shadowed with thought. But built like a warrior too.

The men have licence to search the court. Achilles doesn't need Lycomedes to warn him they have come for him. He must now be only Pyrrha. But these men carry the smell of action. While Deidamia dresses his hair, he smoulders.

The search is over. Nestor and his companions have been through every corner of the palace, questioned every groom, stable-hand, man and boyservant in the place, examined their form and features – and particularly their hands – to see if any might be Peleus' famous son: the boy who kills lions with his hands; who can outrun a deer.

But no one has seen him.

And no one could be him.

Of course they have other business. Nestor invites Lycomedes to contribute some ships to their expedition. Lycomedes feasts the ambassadors with lamb and wine and honey.

The ambassadors in turn have gifts for the court: jars containing the best Achaean wine and promise of much more if a navy is sent.

'We also have pretty gifts for the ladies,' says Odysseus, and word goes out that the women and girls of the court are

to gather. Odysseus fetches in a small chest and begins to
unpack:

> bracelets,
> necklaces,
> rings,
> lengths of fine fabric,
> delicate sandals,
> a little knife,
> mirrors of polished bronze and among them, a shield;
> embroidered girdles. A spear.

He lays them out around him.

'There's something for everyone,' he says. 'Don't hold back.
Each one of you, choose something.'

Gradually they all move forward. Some at first are shy as
does but soon all are engrossed, picking over the gifts,
handling them, passing them between one another, trying
things on. Deidamia has led her friend Pyrrha into the
circle and Pyrrha too experiments with cloth and bracelets.

EEEEEEEEEEIIIIIIIAAAAAEEEEEEAAAAGGGGHHH!!!!!
   Outside: the aching ring of metal on metal and the
unmistakeable sound of a man's breath fleeing his body for
ever.

Achilles is there, the shield already on one arm, the little
knife in the same hand, the spear – ready to fall wherever it
is needed – balanced in the other.

'There you are,' says Odysseus (who has forfeited the life of one of his men to this end).

'I didn't think you could resist a fight. Come with us. There'll be a better one in Troy.'

Two destinies, Thetis said. You can choose.

Stay in the fight and be known – for ever – as the greatest warrior on earth, and your life will be short as the beat of that wing.

Or – if you can be happy without this name – live long and peacefully, farming Peleus' land in Phthia alongside Neoptolemus, the son now growing in Deidamia's womb. Stay, and you will never meet him while you live.

Choose.

The Choice

Deidamia's slender boy-lover has grown into a man, his large body moulded by action.

On action.

On action.

For nine years he has followed the flame, not pausing to remember his mother's words.

He leads his Myrmidons – the ant-men – into battle, their shields scrumming to make flexible, impenetrable walls. He makes raids – alone or with Patroclus. Cattle, massing like storm to thunder down the slope as you close in.

Then reaction.

Agamemnon pulls rank (the only way he pulls anything) and takes Briseis – the girl who was Achilles' prize.

And Achilles remembers that he can choose. He lays off his men and folds his arms.

The fifty beached orange ships frame a village of soldiers at ease. The Myrmidons – those strong maquis fighters – are at play. They throw dice, wrestle, fish, tell stories. Patroclus and Achilles dance. The sight of this little village with its smoke and easy laughter offends Agamemnon more than he can say. He feels his army sinking deeper with each day that passes. He feels that they, not Troy, are under siege.

The Trojans feel so safe they come down to the beach and kill Greeks there. And Thetis purrs, satisfied that Zeus is avenging her son.

Agamemnon thinks of everything he can to win Achilles back. He will give him the woman now (swearing he hasn't touched her) along with seven more. And any one of his surviving daughters for a wife when they get home. Plus the usual bronze, gold, tripods etc.

Do they really think he is greedy?

The only child of Agamemnon he'd marry is the dead one – the one they offered, then killed. He is ready to sail home. To a long and nameless future.

It's not as if the wounded pride of a son of Atreus was ever his affair.

But Patroclus is tender-hearted. It hurts him to see the wounds of his fellows. He begs Achilles: 'Let me go into battle, dressed in your armour.'

And Achilles lets him.

This armour fits three men and no one else:

Achilles, for whom it was made; Patroclus (who nevertheless cannot lift the great ash spear that goes with it) and … who else? What did you say? *WHO?*

To a Trojan it's a fearful sight: Achilles' armour moving again. Though without the great ash spear.

But Hector – he is the third – is not afraid. He is only disappointed when he comes to peel the armour from Patroclus' body that the smashed flesh inside is not Achilles.

~

HECTOR.

Before there was the name there was the shadow.

The shadow Achilles felt first at Skiros. It teased his own body on to growth. Cell by cell, calling him.

Body for body, each grew.

So that Achilles' armour, stripped from Patroclus, now fits Hector perfectly.

And Achilles no longer has a choice.

Ajax and Menelaus have rescued the poor, heavy, mangled body (they thought it would break as they heaved Patroclus by the armpits while Hector hung on to a foot). Achilles washes the dear flesh. He tells Patroclus he will not sleep till Hector is dead. Nor will he eat.

Achilles of the loud war cry lets out his war cry…

and the Achaeans regroup. Each man of them merry and agile for war.

The Trojans shit themselves.

~

But not even he can go naked into battle and count on winning. Thetis, heavy-hearted, makes him wait; goes to

Olympus to order new armour. When he straps it on he feels himself lifted on wings; when the sun strikes it men are blinded.

The metal is stamped with the future he won't see.

On this day he finds twelve Trojans for Patroclus' funeral pyre. He picks them off easily, before the sun has cleared the mist. His Myrmidons rope them together and drag them off alive. They'll keep.

He moves on towards the river. No Trojan has a chance. He on his own has the strength of one army; the Myrmidons – all their unused power unleashed – are another.

Up to his thighs in the River Scamander.

The River Scamander choking with blood and corpses. A thick, stinking soup; so full of bodies of men and horse, bits of limbs and pikes, mashed hide of shields, it can hardly move.

Scamander longs for the sea. So near he could smell it if it weren't for this stinking freight. If he could only flow to join it, this vile cargo would disperse. Then he could breathe again. But now he is so weighed down, so clogged. Like a dying man he cannot raise his head to meet the longed-for water near his mouth.

But Scamander will not die. He rouses himself from his deepest fundament, draws up his strength . . . and heaves.

And heaves again. A terrible, dry retching as he throws the bits that choke him out onto his banks.

Sodden mangled corpses:

men,

horses,

tackle...

and again he can breathe and flow. Now he will drown the man who has hacked so many sons of Troy into his waters.

When the river roars at him Achilles jumps in, ready to take him on. Scamander clasps him, grabs him by the throat, and rises in a tower over his head.

Like a slab of rock over his head.

Like his funeral pile heaped over his head.

Water, the stuff of his mother, is now so heavy.

She never said this would happen: that he would die like a boy whose boat's turned over, his dead flesh waterlogged, teased apart by fish, buried at last in silt.

And Hector alive.

Summoning all his strength he rears, like Atlas rising to slide the heavens from his back. Moving through water he sees a tree – an elm – its trunk leaning out over the river. He grabs it with one arm and hauls himself up till he has wrapped his legs around. But the weight of Achilles and his heavenly armour is more than the roots of this tree can bear. They try to grip the earth they're dug in, send out new fingers to fasten into the bank. The tree doesn't want to drown either. It clings to the bank but the bank cannot hold on to itself and breaks away, clod by fat clod, ripping the sinews of root and fibre that bound it. It falls away like cake, a new island carried by the rushing river, Achilles still straddling the tree.

Achilles hurls himself towards the open wound of the

bank and the River Scamander gathers itself up into a wall. So high it blots out the sun.

This wall of water comes after Achilles.

ZEUS HELP ME!

The cry hits target. Though Achilles is not his son – *because* Achilles is not his son – Zeus loves him. He sends his brother Poseidon and his grey-eyed brainchild Athene to clasp the man's hands and bear him up. They assure him he *will* kill Hector. Nothing can take this from him.

But Scamander won't let up. His wall of water's poised to crash down even on the gods. Zeus and Athene call on Hephaestus: ask him for fire.

Hephaestus lobs fire down and, for a moment that all who survived will remember for ever, a river of molten flame pours through the sky. As it meets land it roars into a blaze, romping over the heaped bodies that Achilles killed that morning, eating them whole.

Hungry still, it makes for the river; breathes on the water which shrinks, scalded, from its banks.

Scamander – a hot, narrow vein in a bed of baking mud – surrenders.

~

THE TROJAN soldiers – what's left of them – are scuttling back behind the walls. How small they look in flight; men who even yesterday shone with power as they poured across the beach. The women watching from the ramparts see the small wounded dots hauling their way up the hill. Husband, brother, child. Something in the configuration of each moving mark is unmistakeable to eyes made sharp by love. Hephaestus' flames have eaten the dead. But the wounded are brought home on stretchers of shields or dragged, slumped across their companions' shoulders. The dust on the paths is rosy with blood. Men tumble through the gate. Men without arms, men with barely half a face, a hole where the nose was. One unstraps his helmet and, as he tugs it off, the skull flaps back and his brains slide down his neck.

QUICK!

CLOSE THE GATE. ACHILLES IS COMING.

Those who have only heard of Achilles would like to linger for a glimpse, but the men who press in push them back. They bundle their companions through. If only to die inside Troy's walls.

Priam orders them to close the great Scaean Gate before Achilles can reach it.

QUICK!

GET IN!

The huge leaves of the gate are pushed together, the enormous bolts heaved into place. For a moment they breathe in relief. But they know the end has begun.

Then someone says that Hector is still out there. The two of them. Out there.

They needn't have bothered to run. Achilles has no interest in any other Trojan now. He has just seen Hector from the plain – high on a boulder near the ramparts, in full view, surveying the land below.

As if spears, boulders and axes could not be hurled.

As if he were watching the sky for signs of weather.

Achilles reaches the wall and sees Hector outside the gates, an easy spear's flight away. They look at each other and, just for a moment, time stops, eyes blazing into eyes as each takes in the form and splendour of the other and thinks *It's him*. Then Achilles raises the great ash spear and Hector begins to run and the race, which both always knew would one day begin, begins.

Hector's feet are sure. They know these tracks, where they'll find scree, where the ground is firm. As he runs he remembers each part of his life: the bushes and rocks of his boyhood hideouts, the promontory he lay on one full night to learn the stars; the routes of his hunting, his cattle herding, the waterfall he led Andromache to when he wooed her. The stream of Astyanax's first bathing. The shallow rock pools where the women did the laundry before the war. He remembers, his life spread out before him like a giant sheet in the sun, the way ahead narrowing to a tunnel which he runs down.

The rhythm of their steps goes on for ever.

It makes no difference that Achilles does not know the terrain so well. He is strong as a stag. Inexhaustible. Hector can gain no ground. Three times they circle the city. Now Hector scans the walls for armed comrades who might occupy Achilles while he scales the battlements and escapes; but Achilles never lets him get close to the walls.

The Myrmidons press in. Stationed at various points in the circuit they follow Achilles as they can, keeping Hector running, blocking off his escapes. But if one of them raises a spear or a boulder Achilles glares him to a halt. No one will take this kill from him.

Athene is back with him – lucid and swift and not at all out of breath. She tells him again that Hector is his and promises to make him stop. Then, looking like Deiphoebus, she catches up with Hector who takes heart, happy that his dear brother has risked his life to join him. Ready now, he stops in his tracks, and turns.

Again Achilles' eyes meet Hector's. The Myrmidons stand back.

Hector promises an honourable deal: the winner will treat the other's body with respect and allow his people to fetch it for decent burial.

Achilles looks at the man who killed Patroclus and feels the hatred spread through his body, slowly, luxuriously, like cream. A sumptuous hatred that leaves no part of him unfilled.

'No Hector. We meet as animals. What's left of you will go to the dogs.'

He lifts the great ash spear that even Patroclus could not hold. And throws.

Hector ducks. The spear pierces the ground. Immediately, unseen by Hector, Athene tweaks it out and hands it back to Achilles.

Now it is Hector's throw. Achilles' miss has cheered him. He casts his own great spear which lands, dead centre, in Achilles' Olympic shield.

But no god tweaks it out and he has no other spear.

Deiphoebus is nowhere to be seen.

Now he knows he has come to his death. He draws his huge sword and wields it with both hands.

Achilles takes his sword too. After the day's slaughter the divine blade still flashes like a sun. There is all the time he could ever want. He looks Hector over, scanning the armour that fits him so well, searching for a place to insert his blade. Like a lover taking in every inch of his beloved as they lie in the hot sun. All the time he could want, no rush, no fear of missing.

There is one point where the armour does not close over Hector. The tender diamond hollow between the clavicles is naked. Achilles fits his sword's tip here.

Slowly, evenly, the pressure mounting, he pushes.

Father

Only two of the three chariot horses are left. Pedasus has fallen, the outrigger who gallantly kept pace, and only the two immortals remain. This is the twelfth dawn broken by Achilles heaving them into harness. He doesn't even pause to pass a hand over their satin necks. Each dawn for the last eleven days he has hooked great Hector's body like a plough to the back of his chariot. He has threaded a strap through Hector's ankles, thonging them together like fish to be carried. Then he hooks this thong to his car and drags the body, nose bumping down, through the dust. He has done this each morning. Three times each morning they circle the stone barrow built for Patroclus. A modest barrow, built to tide Patroclus over till the not far time when he and Achilles will lie together again under something more fit.

Achilles has not slept since his oblivion on the beach after the funeral. Then he was out, face down in the sand by the raked-over ashes. Patroclus had let him rest. But not for long. For the last eleven days and nights Achilles' eyes have burned in their sockets so his men are afraid to look at them. But he doesn't see his men. He doesn't notice Briseis, more friendless than ever with Patroclus gone. She creeps around like an unowned kitten, fending for herself as best she can. He doesn't even see the barrow where Patroclus' ashes lie, though round and round and round he goes. He has eyes for one man only: that huge body, winched up by the heels each day at dawn, which will not rot, which will not stop being beautiful.

When he had finished killing Hector the Myrmidons had each had a go, killing him again and again. They took it in turns to shove in a spear. Some jabbed; others wiggled, getting the feel of the man, till Hector's body, stripped of the armour he had stolen from Patroclus, was ugly, squelching pulp. Now all those wounds are sealed. Achilles has never seen a body so perfect. It has only one mark: a stain like a kiss at Hector's throat.

On this twelfth morning he is making for Hector when Thetis appears. She interposes her immortal self between Hector and her son and Achilles, wanting to see round her, is forced to see her. She takes a hand in both her cool ones; holds his head and kisses his hammering brow.

'Child,' she says, 'this has to stop.'

At the same moment Iris goes to Priam. His eyes are raw with weeping; tears have washed stripes in the filth on his face. When Iris finds him he is moaning and rubbing dung from the stables into his hair – as if it were ointment.

The goddess touches his shoulder.

'Priam, this cannot go on. Zeus has sent me to tell you you are to go to Achilles with gifts. He will give up Hector's body in return. Take your chariot, a waggon for a bier, and one driver. You won't need a guard.'

Hecuba thinks her husband has gone mad. The plan is certain death. The end of Troy – sure enough with Hector gone – a matter now of days.

'If you're so sure Zeus is with you, ask him for a sign.'

Priam is sure. Outside with his waggon and Idaeus, his old herald, to drive it, he offers Zeus wine and prays to the thinker god to send his bird. They hear the heavy wings of Zeus' eagle and see the bird riding the air to the right. Falling under its huge shadow Hecuba's heart clears.

All day Achilles has sat with Hector, watching him, not taking his eyes off him for a second. He doesn't move; only a muscle in his cheek tightens from time to time.

Cassandra looks down through the dusk from the ramparts of Troy as the mule-drawn waggon sets off with the cart behind it. The great eagle stays close to the travellers, holding the waggon as tight in its gaze as a gull holds a boat soon to land its trawl.

Zeus sends Hermes to guide them in the form of a Myrmidon. It is a warm dusk and mist rises high from Scamander's banks. Priam and Idaeus have stopped to water the animals. When they see the Myrmidon shoulder through the mist towards them Priam's hand moves towards his sword.

'The royal Priam. Away from Troy so late! Have you deserted her now you've lost Hector?'

Priam flinches. The god goes on:

'You'll know me for one of Achilles' men. Don't be afraid.

I have a father your age. But what are you doing here with this old man? Do you want to get killed?'

Priam is not afraid. When Hermes tells him that Hector's body is as firm and as beautiful as if gods had embalmed it – and this in spite of Achilles' daily ritual of insult – his heart soars. Hector's piety has not gone unnoticed. He rummages for a moment beneath the waggon's wicker cover and comes up with a heavy golden beaker.

Hermes refuses the gift, pretending to think it a bribe.

'But I will guide you past the sentries and take you to the lord Achilles. These nights he never sleeps.'

Hermes puts the sentries to sleep. Idaeus' waggon with four mules drawing it, Priam's chariot with Hermes riding it, move as peacefully across the Achaean trench as two farm carts entering town on market day.

When they reach Achilles' compound, fenced-off with a high palisade, his ship moored nearby, Hermes reveals himself to Priam. Only a god – or Achilles – could, single-handed, slip back the bolt that fastens the fence.

~

ACHILLES SITS motionless, a table of untasted food in front of him. Priam sinks before him and embraces his knees.

Imagine: the mighty Priam crouched before you like a child.

Gently Achilles removes his hands from the old man's clasp. For a moment it looks as if he will stroke the long white hair, it is so like the hair of his own father whom he has not seen these nine years since he set sail with Phoenix for Troy. Huge sobs break from Achilles as he thinks of

Peleus, ageing at home in Phthia, uncomforted by his son. And Priam? He thinks of Hector – of what else has he thought these twelve days? – who was like no one else on earth and whom no one could match but this man.

The two men hold each other and weep: for those they have lost, for those who will lose them, for all the men gone down in the slow years of this wasteful war.

~

WHEN THE time for tears is past Achilles raises Priam to his feet and fetches him a fine, inlaid chair.

'You're brave, to come here unguarded. My men are like wolves. I kept them out of the fight too long. Now they've tasted blood again.'

'It's Hector's body I've come for. There was no question of fear.'

This irritates Achilles.

'Don't give me that. It takes three young, strong men to knock back the bolt on my gate. I know you've been helped by a god. I've had my instructions too. It's Zeus' wish that I give you the body and that's why you'll get it.'

He turns away; the muscle in his cheek at work again.

He leaves Priam seated and takes two of his women (not Briseis – two others) to where he keeps Hector when he's not dragging him in the dust. He glares at Hector accusingly, as if a pact had been broken, then snaps into command, telling the women to wash the body and be sure to rinse away every grain of dirt. He is emphatic about this – as if the dirt he's dragged Hector through had actually clung, whereas Hector shines through it, shunning the dirt as oil shuns water.

When the body is clean the women are to anoint it.

Priam must be kept from seeing the body till it is time for him to take it. If he sees it now he will want to kill Achilles. Achilles knows how strong old men can be but it is his own strength he fears. If Priam's hands go for his throat he can buck him off. The hard thing is stopping there. He sees Priam crashing to the floor and the outrage in his eyes. He feels his own shame.

'Mother,' he murmurs, 'cool me down.'

And he feels Thetis' sea-cool hand pass over him.

He returns to Priam's gifts, noting their splendour with satisfaction.

He picks out one of the softest robes and goes out again. Priam half rises to follow; stops when he meets Achilles' gaze.

The women have oiled Hector and laid him out. The power that shines from him is nearly blinding. Achilles hands the garment to the women, hoping it will veil the brightness which tells him the gods love Hector, even in death.

He supports the great shoulders as Automedon and Alcimus help him bear Hector to the waggon. He looks on his conquered enemy for the last time.

Priam wants to rush out to the bier but Achilles restrains him.

'There is a time for everything.

'Whatever the occasion a man needs food and rest,' (*this* from Achilles!) 'even Niobe needed to eat at last, though for ten days after her children's slaughter she neither ate nor slept. Tonight you're my guest. You must eat and I must serve you.'

He goes outside to his small flock – their meat and milk for his household use – and takes the finest and whitest-woolled and slaughters it. He slings the carcass over his neck and carries it into the hut where he works quickly and neatly, cutting flesh away from mantling fat. Then he and his men thread the meat onto spits which they thrust into the fire to sizzle and drop their juices. Baskets of bread are passed around and each man helps himself, Achilles helping Priam to the choicest pieces until he can take no more. Wine is drunk, the best of Achilles' store, most delicious to Achilles and Priam who have fasted and watched these twelve days.

Filled with the comfort of food and wine, Priam is at peace. The grief and hatred that have been driving him, step down. Pain slides off and his limbs relax and warm to being at rest. He looks at his host and finds him magnificent. He admires, though cannot like, Achilles' nerved face, each feature outlined clear. The huge hands that can fashion as well as place a spear.

Achilles too is soothed. The Fury that has gripped him, worried at him, gnawed him, thwacked him against her cavern's walls, has put him down. He looks at his guest and admires the breadth of the man; the stature which age has not shrunk up. He senses what real power those sceptre-wielding hands still hold.

But Priam is tired and craves a bed. Achilles' guard goes up.

'You and your herald must sleep outside – you mustn't be seen here. But tell me, how many days will you need to prepare for Hector's funeral? I will lay off the troops for as long as you need.'

Priam asks for eleven days for Trojans to go safely into the mountains to collect wood for the pyre. For nine days they will mourn in their homes, on the tenth day they will hold the funeral and on the eleventh build the barrow. Achilles grasps Priam's wrist as a pledge of his faith, and the two men part to sleep.

The stars stick out like jewels.

Priam's sleep is deep and dreamless in the high bed prepared by Achilles' women. He is woken by Hermes.

'Priam! Priam, get up. How can you sleep with your enemies all around! Hurry now. We must go while it's still dark.'

Priam and Idaeus scramble down from their beds. Quietly they untether the horses and harness them to the chariot. The horses are restive and eager to go – their snorts and pacings break the quiet, but the night is always full of sounds – the sheep bells clanking and the wind in the rigging of the great Achaean fleet. They yoke the mules to the bier and Idaeus climbs up to drive them while Priam takes his horses' reins. Hermes speeds ahead, slips back the bolt and climbs up next to Priam. The horses prick back their ears when the Olympian takes the reins.

This night – like every night – fires light the plain and from afar it looks another sky, mirroring the clearer heavenly one in its more muddied light. As they pass the trench and begin to cross the plain fire-light bruises the air with reddish smoke. They thread between the fires, feeling the heat from each in turn like a pulse. As they pass, Hermes puts each vigilant sentry to sleep.

But Cassandra stays vigilant. She has watched ever since her father set off; saw him and Idaeus wind their way across the scrubby plain and now (though she does not see Hermes slide down from his seat and head off) she's the first to see the laden bier return.

She runs down from the battlements and cries,

'Hector has come home!'

And Achilles wakes from his sleep, face down, one arm slung over Briseis' back.

Cut Off

Listen. Achilles never wanted to die.

Don't think because Patroclus is dead he wants to die.

His hair has grown again. The thick auburn lock he cut and laid on Patroclus' corpse. (The other Myrmidons did the same till Patroclus looked like a great tawny eagle covered with soft plumes.) But that hank of hair which went down with his friend is a forerunner. Part of him, hostage in the underworld.

What does he love now, enough to hold him here?

He loves the light. Twice as much as before.

At times he seems almost merry. The Achaeans feel themselves renewed: they are fighting with the strength they had at first, before the ten years wore them down.

Achilles is now more mortal than ever. Knowing it, he fights like a god and Zeus is as proud of him as if he'd seeded him.

He and Patroclus once said they would bring down Troy alone. Troy and all her allies. Now as he fights he is like a fire in summer.

He has heard stories about the women fighters. Some say

they have seen them. 'Like Furies,' they say, 'like she-wolves.' A pack will stalk, round up and set upon a victim, each taking a part in the kill, each – so they say – tasting the flesh of their prey and smearing herself with his blood.

What is it makes him know it's a woman he sees – that mounted figure looking out over the plain from the cliff? He knows, as surely as if he were next to her, breathing the scent of her flesh.

And he knows that he will meet her.

Not on horseback – though she is mounted – and not encased in his heavenly armour. When he goes to find her he is dressed lightly as if he were going to a wrestling bout, or a diver in search of pearls. He takes only a small dagger tucked into the band he wears at his waist.

He does not make for the promontory where he saw her looking out but a little way inland where the bushes grow tight and give good cover. She must ride this way, unless her horse can fly.

As he waits he listens. If it is true they hunt in packs there will be others.

This is a quiet place, away from the knots of fighting which form, collapse and reassemble hour after hour after hour. Here the only sounds are the shifting hum of the bees grazing among thyme and myrtle; the slight breath of the wind. Chiron taught him how to attend to its shiftings. He can lay his mind open like a bird and ride wide-winged upon the thermals.

He hears her horse – twigs snapping, bushes pressed, the

quiet tearing of fibres as turf is crushed. Almost silently he climbs up into a strong tree – a chestnut – and waits.

Penthiseleia, Queen of the Amazons.

She was watching the sea which today is breaking and breaking in little white waves, each a gash in the sea's body, a wound which heals till the skin breaks open again somewhere else. She has no taste for this war of Priam's, no feel for its arbitrary rhythms. The battles she and her women excel in are concentrated and unremitting till the end. This war lacks definition; the allies don't know each other; there are too many languages. They cannot move as one. This morning she has ridden away from her warriors to rinse her mind clean.

Achilles waits till she has passed below, then swings his body forward to land exactly and neatly behind her. He has dropped like this in a hundred ambushes, dragging riders, sometimes galloping, to the ground. This one he clasps tight. He holds his dagger to her throat... but he does not pull her down.

The moment she knows this enemy behind her she jabs her elbows back into his ribs and would spin round to fight him were it not for the blade tightening at her throat. Defying it, she calls to her horse and drives her heels sharply into the stallion's flanks so he rears up whinnying, vertical as a pillar. Achilles is not shaken off and Penthiseleia calls out again. In spite of the bushes, in spite of the narrowness and difficulty of the path, they begin to gallop.

Careful not to slacken the closeness of knife to throat but not tightening it either, Achilles presses the Amazon's upper body with his own, down upon the horse's neck so he lies across her like a shield as they plunge through the thick growth of trees and bushes.

They come to open ground: the sun on his back again he straightens, drawing her with him. On surer ground the Amazon's horse gallops more freely, making for the camp where he has grazed, where the mare who foaled him grazes now.

Soon they will be visible to the other Amazons. Penthiseleia knows they will pick off the man with their arrows. Now as never before she must trust their skill. It is his neck they must hit – or his side, but neck is better. The slightest misjudgement could wound her or the horse.

Achilles knows he could pull her from the horse at any moment. On this open plain he could easily break their fall. He stays because there is a pleasure in galloping like this, holding her close. Two breasts – the rumours aren't true – and narrow hips. A waist, lean and flexible. He enjoys the smell of her strong sweat. No taint of fear in it.

He is eager to rip the life out of any man or woman who might have wished Hector more alive than Patroclus; but this strong-legged woman did not care for Hector. The Amazons, like most of Troy's allies, can have no more interest in Paris' quarrel with Menelaus than he and Patroclus once had. When he saw her, looking out to sea, he thought of Iphigeneia. Only this one is hot where the other – vowed to Artemis – was blade-cool.

For Penthiseleia too there is comfort in his belly meeting her back. She is as easy with his movements as she is with her horse whose limbs are almost her own.

But her mind tells her otherwise: tells her to oppose this man and kill him.

She must do it herself. Her sisters must not see her powerless like this, a man's arm pinning hers to her body while his other holds a knife to her throat – holds it so close he could trim her neck like a piece of wood.

If she could meet him head on she could fight him.

When she turns her head he withdraws the knife a fraction. Not much, not enough to prevent a fine necklace of blood pricking out around her throat. Riding behind her, pressing up close, has aroused him, and the sight of her face, cheek-bones soaring like the wings of swallows, makes him want her more.

In turning she thought to shove him to the ground where she'd fall on him and quickly stab him, but it is he who drags her with him from the horse and grapples her close as they break their fall in the grass. She thrusts a hand into the roots to stay herself; finds a small sharp stone which she rapidly prises from the ground and palms.

Achilles has taken his knife from her throat. He holds her now to steady her, not to restrain her. He looks at her blazing, furious face and laughs, glad that she exists.

'My Queen,' he says, pulling her to him.

The words are nonsense to her; a foreign babble. Though

her back still sings with the memory of him pressing her she will not submit.

He draws her closer, puts his tongue to the wound at her throat; iron of blood mixed with salt of sweat. His tongue will scour it clean.

AAAAAAIIIIIIIEEEEEE!!!

A sharp, dangerous pain flames up his spine. He twists to throw off whatever it is that attacks him, pushes her hands away with a force which might snap her forearms, sees the bloody little nose of flint she's been using to excavate the base of his spine.

Now he pins her down, all his hurt, unmet tenderness turned to indignation. He bends back her fingers to make her release the flint and she makes those fingers her weapons, tearing his face, stabbing at eyes. His knee bent across her ribs, holding her down, he covers her face with one hand, the heel of the other hand cradling the back of her skull, and pushes. He feels her body trying to arch beneath him, the resistance of her head as she struggles to free it. He pushes on. Pushes and then, with practised economy, twists. He holds her a little longer. Waiting for the turmoil of the body to quieten. Waiting for it to be over.

His hand fits her face perfectly; its mask. He peels it away with a sense of wonder, as if what lies beneath his palm is something he has made and never seen: like a potter when he lifts a piece from the cooled furnace, or a metal worker, brushing away sand. He peels away his hand and finds beneath it a face he could love with all his heart.

Her horse is not far away. He catches it and lifts the body of his new love across the stallion's back. When he too is on the horse he holds her body to him. He will take her to the sea – to the place she was gazing at, where the sea is clean, not churning with slaughtered bodies.

~

THE DIFFICULTY, amidst all this slaughter, is to hold on to what is distinct – catch the little gust of a dying breath, follow the brightness of one face before it is eaten by dark. Sometimes, in battle, he sees a face, the curve of a cheek, the way the light catches it, and he follows it, makes it his guide to lead him deeper into the mess.

So Polyxena's face, pale as the moon.

Always, throughout his life, bright faces moving away, disappearing behind curtains: his mother taken back in a curtain of water, Iphigeneia wrapped in flames, Patroclus' face as it speaks to him these nights, folded in darkness. When Polyxena's form is swallowed by the curtain at the entrance to the temple, he must go after. Layer on layer are here. Following this girl he follows them all – his mother, Iphigeneia, Penthiseleia, Patroclus – yes, and Hector too. He will pursue them all to the vanishing point but he must not lose sight of her.

She is going to Apollo's temple. She carries a pitcher of clean water and intends to scour and rinse the temple till there is no mote of dust for the god's sun shafts to light upon. Nothing must get in his way. Apollo's light must fill this place till it is tight with power.

Paris is in there, taking shelter. At least Apollo loves him and repairs his bruised pride. It is hard to be so hated and despised – even by Helen these days. He likes to think he resembles Apollo: young(ish), lithe, good-looking, fairly good at singing, a crack archer. Forget the healing.

The fact is, Apollo has no feelings either way about Paris. Who? Oh, *him*. Yes, amazing what looks do.

But Achilles. Apollo hates Achilles. He has every reason to; for Achilles – not even a god – excels in everything that he, divine Apollo, is good at. Achilles is the best musician, the best archer. He is also – using only mortal means – the best physician: as good at dressing wounds as making them. And Zeus, Apollo's father, loves Achilles as if he were his own.

When Achilles plunges over the threshold it is simple to take aim; simple to nudge Paris into doing the gestures – lift bow, notch arrow, release – simple to bend the flight of Paris' arrow so it no longer goes for the heart but the left heel, where Achilles' life is strangely gathered and held.

Following a face in a crowd. A face bright as the moon. The crowd closes in, darkening the way, getting between him and the face he must find and follow. The face of Thetis, Iphigeneia, Penthiseleia, Polyxena. The face of Deidamia, of Patroclus, Hector. Stumbling now, for it is dark and he's lost sight of the face in all the throng, he feels an army's worth of arrows rain down on him. His flesh is like a beach when the rain drums down in hard vertical lines, pushing its way through the sand, drenching every grain. These arrows pierce each cell of him, breaking the walls. He is carried on the river of his own blood, mighty as Scamander, storming the channels of his body. He is carried to the place where the river is sucked into a twist and the other river begins.

GONE

Urn

They fell on your carcass like jackals. Those who would not have dared to come near you in life, suddenly very brave. Everyone wanted to get a look, a feel. They plan to boast about this for the rest of their lives, which for most of them is not long.

'You should have seen the look in his eyes. Not fear. Surprise.'

'I touched one of his hands – twice the size of mine. Little reddy-gold hairs on the back of it.'

'So young, his face.'

Moments after you were felled – slamming into the ground like a huge tree – there was chaos. They did not want to let you go, these Trojans who had got you so suddenly. So undeservedly. But Odysseus and Ajax arrived, wielding their broad swords.

Ajax hooked his arms under your shoulders as Odysseus, fierce as a dog, drove back the Trojan scavengers. He snarled, menacing on all sides, laying about him with the butt of his spear then twirling it round to stab. He plied it nimbly, as if it were part of him.

Then Ajax, his own great body filled with sorrow, lifted you. He kneeled to insert his left shoulder under the place where your body folds and then, with a stamp and a loud exhalation, staggered to his feet.

Yes. Great Ajax staggered under the weight of you.

Now your body has been washed. Briseis has done this, her exile's heart breaking, tears mixing with the clean water. She has dried you with her long hair and with linen. She has crushed herbs into the oil she anoints you with: hyssop, myrtle, juniper, rosemary. Maquis herbs that smell of Pelion's shrubby mountainside in the sun.

Your glistening body, healed of its single wound, is laid out on the bier.

You saw how it would be when you buried Patroclus.

One by one your Myrmidons approach you. Each man saws at his hair with his sword's edge and lays this tribute on you. Each man is weeping.

After the Myrmidons, the generals. Even Agamemnon weeps as he bows his head beside you, ashamed now of his greed. Your body under this soft piled blanket of black and brown, russet and gold. The wind detaches and lifts some of the locks. Bright hairs separate themselves and float in the air like strange insects. Sea horses of the air.

~

A TERRIBLE SOUND. A great wailing. A keening that never seems to exhaust itself but which moves in waves, each fuller than the one before. The sea has altered. Where before it was one bright blue, broken only by the myriad jagged flashes of sunlight, it is darker now. Purple waves, green ones, waves of a deeper blue roll in, one on top of the other, lipping it, chasing it, waves pouring in as if to flood the beach. As if racing to drown every creature that remains on the beach.

The sudden darkening of the waves makes the men look up at the sky, expecting to see signs of a storm. They find unbroken blue. The mild wind continues to lift the locks of hair – they hang in the air like leaves on an autumn day. Yet still the sound grows and the small waves race in. Some meteorological catastrophe must be at hand: a whirl-wind, a twister, or else a tidal wave once these flat little waves have gathered force. The keening must be the sound of the wind whipping in the distance. They have heard of such phenomena.

In spite of the strangeness of the sea, some men make for the ships. The instinct of sailors who want home.

Chaos on the beach: as before a storm when dry leaves swirl on the forest floor in separate conflicting eddies. The generals attempt to impose some kind of order but it is hard for them to be heard.

Only the Myrmidons to a man keep close to you. Not one of them will desert his beloved commander.

Nestor sees what is happening and has a word with Odysseus. There is no storm coming. Achilles' mother and her sisters are arriving from the sea to be present at the funeral. He speaks quietly – his old voice cannot carry as Menelaus' does – but once he has spoken calm settles again.

With calm a sense of wonder spreads. Now the fear has gone the warriors stand in silence, listening to the subtle harmonies that make up this keening.

The sound is the sound that would happen if every fish in a silver shoal had its own fine note. An intricacy of sound, a close-stitched cloth. Each fish a needle darting over and under, under and over, till the cloth is tight. Each needle a note, taking its place in the vast canopy of sound that spreads itself out over their heads. This pliant, seam-free cloth of shot silk which encloses them unfurls, interposing itself between them and the sky.

Many who are there have never knowingly met gods before. Their hearts, open already with grief, salute the marvellous happening.

The air too seems to stand to attention and within it, each mote of light moves. Each mote twirls and dances, like the bright lifted sections of hair. Each mote sings.

Then something happens which all can discern. The sea is suddenly crowded with silvery creatures. Not like fish. Bigger. More like a large colony of seals making its way up onto the shore; heaving, sliding, pulling, arcing. A flickering mass of gleaming bodies, dark as ore or mottled and luminous. Some are pale as honey. Each one in an ecstasy of movement.

As they arrive on the beach the song thickens. Soon they are all here: Thetis, her sisters, and those nine daughters of Zeus and Mnemosyne, the Muses. They stand together on the shore and sing and their song burns in the veins of all who hear it. It is stronger than unmixed wine.

~

THETIS HAS been busy on Olympus, rousing the Muses; moving through the earth's salt waters in search of her sisters. As an immortal she can go wherever she likes, in any shape she chooses.

But what is the point of immortality if your child does not share it? The freedom of Heaven and earth is a small gift to one who wishes to go nowhere except into Hell where she cannot get in. It is impossible for her: the wrong density. Ordinary living mortals have more to do with the dead than the likes of her. They see ghosts; hear the dead's commands. Thetis will never hear the dead Achilles ask for Polyxena any more than she saw Patroclus when his ghost came to visit her still-alive son.

For seventeen days and nights they mourn; mortals and immortals together. If any human there doubts the reality of divine grief, the cries of Thetis set them right. Terrible to hear, they pierce the tight mosaic of the Muses' song. Those who hear feel as if the sea is emptying itself having scoured its floor. That strange creatures will be cast up on the beach.

While others sit hunched, concentrated in grief, Thetis is restless, pacing the beach as she wails, or darting forwards to break through the other mourners and get close to the bier. Nothing can tire her. She has will and energy for any quest or task. She would look for a flower in a desert or search the beaches of the world for one particular small stone. She would welcome any hard duty as easy compared with the difficulty that faces her now when nothing she can do will bring him back.

All she has is the jar.

A beautiful jar. Gold. Hammered by a god. Embossed with scenes of hunting. Hephaestus had insisted that she take it at the same time as she fetched the armour.

'You will need this later,' he said.

She had taken it without question – not even wanting to look at it. She'd wedged it under her chin on top of the heaped armour and busied herself with the awkwardness of carrying so much metal. It took a lot of care to get it all down to earth without a scratch.

Only when she and her freight had arrived safely did she begin to examine the jar. She traced each scene with her finger, following it through, saw with a sense of building dread that every scene ended in the same way. She recognised – how could she not? – the shape of the jar. The urn. She wrapped it in lengths of protective silk and put it away.

Now Thetis, take it out. Its time has come.

Before the body is burnt it is anointed again. A thick paste of oil and honey now mantles him. The oil will make the flames burn hotter. For several days men have set out for the higher ground with axes and returned dragging wood for the pyre. The pyre now stands like a giant hive. Taller than a house; an intricate mesh of branches. At its base they have thrust fir cones to help it catch fire.

Twelve of the finest and fattest sheep have been slaughtered and lodged in the pyre. Plus ten handsome, dewlapped steers, their large tongues lolling from lifeless mouths.

It is a delicate task to lift Achilles from the bier and carry him to the top of the pyre. Ajax – who still hopes for the armour – is the proud and sorrowing bearer. He climbs the ladder propped against the arranged wood slowly lest the whole pile topple. It has been well made, like a good dry wall, and while the odd branch gives way the whole is well knit and holds.

Automedon puts the brand to the pyre. Thetis, who once lovingly seared her sons in flame, gasps in pain as the whole thing goes up. Automedon ducks and runs from the almost instant heat. To the sea nymphs the force of the fire is like a scalding wall. Only Thetis braves it. She runs around it, screaming, her dark figure silhouetted against the flames. Some see the black gash of her mouth but the sound of her screams is swallowed by the roar of the flames; the crackings and burstings of wood and flesh and bones.

Night falls. The pyre still blazes, lighting the sky. Soldiers, dressed in their battle gear, file past, firelight burnishing the bronze of their armour. Armed Myrmidons dance with slow and warlike steps to the grave plucked note of the lyre. As they pass they smell the burning flesh. Roasting meat of cattle, sheep and man.

When daylight comes the fire has burnt down. A thick mound of pale dust remains.

Automedon is the first to wade in. Using the flat of his two-handled sword he beats down the dust then, with the blade's edge, he breaks open the last glowing parcels of cinders which exhaust themselves and expire.

When he has gone over it all and the remains of the pyre

lie spread out like a field, Thetis walks in. She sets to work like a gleaner, her bare feet paddling in the soft dust, winnowing the ashes with her hands, gathering bones in the tunic which she holds in an apron before her. Some pieces are thin and dry as sycamore keys or the husk of a chrysalis when the winged creature has gone. She finds the long bones first: femur and tibia, the graceful fibula. The joints are still intact, cartilage shrunk like knobs of resin. Then she picks out the bones of the arms – humerus, radius, ulna. Not hard to find; they are so large, the bones which could move faster than a stag.

She holds the twelve long bones of his body across her arms like wands of peeled wood. They are curiously light now the fire has sucked out their moisture. Light as charcoal and as fragile. It is habit as much as anything that holds them in their shapes. It will not take much to break them into dust. She sets down her load on a clean cloth before returning.

Next she finds the beautiful scapulae. So fine, they are almost transparent. She runs a finger along the delicate shelf of one, clearing it of powdery dust. This could be the beginning of a wing. The column of vertebrae, the spinal cord that threaded this necklace of armour now melted away. The circuit of the pelvis is intact. It makes a strange cincture with its buckle at the pubis. Now she collects the ribs like a precious bundle of kindling. The clavicles – first bones that formed in her womb – her womb now aching as it remembers how it was to carry him. She winnows the grey dust from the small bones that gave form to the spear-wielding hands, the swift and steady feet. She gathers them all and cradles them. They are hardly as heavy as the baby she once held. Much lighter than the armour she collected from heaven to protect him.

But the great helmet of his skull she does not take yet.

It is Machaon, the surgeon, who follows Thetis into the heart of the ash-field, who lifts the skull of Achilles from the dust. He wipes the dust from it and gazes with humble reverence into the dark hollows that housed the eye-pits. He walks over to Thetis. Gently he sets the skull down at the top of her bundle of bones.

Like the jar which Hephaestus gave her she has to hold it in place with her chin to keep it from rolling off.

For a long time she does not move. She stands, bare feet buried in soft ash, as in a field of snow. She looks alone, like a child who must cross a wilderness unescorted. No one who sees her now can remember that she is divine. They all pity her and stand back as she makes her way out of the ash-field with slow, careful steps.

She knows what she must do and knowing is a relief. She sets down all the bones on a spread cloth, laying them out as if she would make another man of them.

But she keeps the skull; tucks it in to the front of her robe as if she were suckling it and takes it with her as she goes to fetch the jar.

It gives her a grim little pleasure to recall that the smith god made it. That this jar of chased gold is undoubtedly the finest funerary urn in existence.

She remembers that her son wanted his bones to be mixed with the bones of Patroclus. Automedon has remembered this too and has been at work exhuming Patroclus' urn. It is an earthenware pot and breaks open easily when struck. The desiccated bones have turned to porous fragments and it is hard to distinguish them from the other fragments – dust and bits of urn – which he carries to Thetis in a bronze bowl. With Thetis he feeds these fragments in through the mouth of the golden urn, then pours in the sediment of clinker.

Now it is Achilles' turn. Thetis handles these bones on her own, knowing how soon they will break up and be indistinguishable from Patroclus'. She feels what each one is and was before she lets it go.

Lastly she removes the skull from her bodice. She cradles it in her hands and then, as Automedon watches in wonder, seems in a moment to unmake it. For as she takes her hands away the skull tumbles into pieces, its separate bones revealed.

There is one bone, shaped like a bird in flight.

Fire

Thetis had cherished a mother's dream for her son:
that he, and not Menelaus, would take Helen for his prize.

They were so well-matched.

One mortal parent, one divine.

The most beautiful with the best.

She knew that Achilles had dreamed of Helen: dreams
that chilled him with their brilliance, like dreams of a waste
of snow. He had woken from those dreams exhausted and
told no one, not even Patroclus, about this nightly irritant
of beauty. Seeking it again he'd made songs, plucking the
strings of his lyre like a cat flexing its claws. He wanted to
excise the bright, unwelcome pearl that troubled him.

And Helen? Did she ever think of him?

What she liked best about him was his absence. The fact
that he was not there at Sparta with the rest of them –
Odysseus, Idomeneus, Elephenor, Menelaus. All pressing in
on her. All wanting her. Achilles' indifference sat on her so
lightly it was almost like love.

When she dreamed of him his body stood out like a cut
jewel against a ground of flame.

Even in the egg she'd felt alone. Cut off. No mother's heart-
beat to ride on; no umbilicus to tether her. Just what was

needed to build a perfect human form. Yolk and shelter.

Locked in the hot, albumen-filled dark Helen could hear the chirruping of Castor and Polydeuces on the other side: their contentment, their togetherness. She afloat in her separate compartment.

Then there was the moment when there was no longer enough room and she found herself pushing, pressing down with her right heel, her whole being concentrated in that place, till something gave.

The sensation of air on her wet leg.

Castor and Polydeuces still muttering to each other in their velvety white sac.

She was ten when Theseus broke in. Her thin, sunned body – a source of pleasure and strength, the place where she lived – made tiny and bruised under his hands. Bones that had sung their green strength in her, turned delicate and raw as the bones of a bird devoured.

When Theseus broke in she silently slipped out; back into the shell she could summon from that instant. It became a bivouac she could watch from. What she watched that first time was a big man with gleaming eyes and a red, wet mouth at the heart of his beard. He came up to her from behind to seize the proud bones that rose like little hills at each side of her belly. Then his hands grasped lower, tugging her apart like the halves of an apricot. Then not his hand but the blind brute of his penis, cramming itself in wherever it could.

Where had they been, her brilliant brothers, to let this happen?

With each other of course.

When Castor and Polydeuces wrestled together she would hurl herself between them like a small, golden-haired meteor. Not trying to stop their fighting but to prise open a space in their intimacy and put herself in. If the twins were two lobes of a single heart, she wanted to be *its* heart. Heart of their heart.

But they were not there when Theseus broke in – though they swore to protect her ever after (and honed her wrestling skills so she was equal with Sparta's best). They are not there now that Hector lies dead and she walled in with those who desire her and hate her.

She thinks, 'I am the loneliest person on earth.'

Men lining up for her.

Having ideas about her.

Fingering her in their thoughts while they finger themselves.

They paste her with their thoughts till there is no air left to breathe.

Not one of them has ever seen her.

Only Hector saw her. Saw loneliness rather than beauty. He, like her, taut with the expectations and hopes of others. So at one with Andromache he lacked curiosity about other women – even the loveliest – as women. He spent time with Helen in the months before the war, before the Greeks arrived. It was Hector who taught her Troy's language.

On the day that he was killed she lost her only friend. If they had stripped her and left her on coastal rocks when the sea was high and raging she could not have felt more exposed.

~

SHE KNOWS they are waiting for her to grow old.

'You're like the rest of us – flesh like curd, pouchy skin, teeth gone brown and rotten. See now if you get what you want.'

She wants them to leave her alone.

But the lovely tautness of her flesh never slackens. Her skin continues to exhale light. Maybe the albumen did it. Or having Zeus for a father. The fact is that nothing that happens to her – nothing that has happened to her – shows.

And that is enough to make them hate her. Her beauty is like a smooth wall which resists all impressions. Paint will not stick to it, neither will mud. You cannot hack into it to make your mark. It makes you feel like you don't exist. It makes you imagine all the things you would do to her, all the ways you could hurt her, so she'd eventually notice you and look like you'd touched her.

And they hate her for that too: for the terrible things she leads them to think of.

Theseus,

Menelaus,

Paris.

Each more inventive than the last in his futile attempts to mark her.

~

THERE ARE Trojans who speak of the time when they saw her close – maybe at an upstairs window, or shaking a rug at a door; perhaps she even smiled. Others have only seen her far off, high on the battlements in her finery for the monthly showings Paris insisted on. Then they had to curl their fists up into funnels and look through the small apertures they made. Seeing such beauty (or imagining they did for she was a long way off) they cheered and their cheers were in Paris' ears as he fucked her. He needed others to want her to want her.

But no one thinks she is worth the death of Hector. Now when people see her they suck their teeth.

There is no place for her grief at Hector's funeral. She is quiet in her despair amidst the wailing and the clamour, watching from the citadel of herself. She does not hate Achilles for killing him but the dreams of flame increase and the form of Achilles grows smaller within the flames; as if he is vanishing and the whole world becoming fire.

When Paris shoots him she takes no pleasure in it.

~

PARIS IS the next to be dead. Philoctetes shoots him through the eye with Heracles' bow, making a mess of that handsome face. She is passed like a tasty bone from son of Priam to son of Priam. Deiphoebus is next in line.

Loneliness draws her, early, while it is still dark, to stroke the flanks of the great wooden horse, parked and abandoned outside Troy's gates. She has guessed its secret. Senses that it is full and waiting to hatch.

She feels an exile's longing to hear her own language spoken again and calls to each of the men crouched inside:

Odysseus, Diomedes, Antielus, Euryplos, Eumelos, Eurydamas, Pheidippos, Leoneus, Meriones, Philoctetes, Meges.

Neoptolemus, Achilles' flame-haired son, newly arrived from Skiros.

Menelaus, her lawful husband.

She whispers to each of them, tenderly, caressingly, with the voice of each man's wife. A life spent watching, listening, has made her flawless in mimicry.

Odysseus, hearing the dark honey of his own Penelope, yearns to reply but suspects a duplicity which is equal to his own. He holds back and silently restrains the others, clamping a hand over Antielus' mouth, putting a dagger's point to his throat.

When he hears her Menelaus knows that he will not be able to kill her as he'd planned. He almost giggles with pleasure as he remembers how she made him feel. His cock thickens and his fear of present danger grows smaller.

Yet the voice he hears is no more her own than the voice of Penelope heard by Odysseus. What each man hears in her now is what each man who looks at her sees: his own desire reflected.

She turns back and remounts the hill to the palace.

She had whispered like this in the egg to her brothers. They had not answered either.

~

THE HORSE breaks open, a limb sticks out, then another one, till the whole form of a man slithers to earth. Man after man pouring out; dark, silent worms, crawling from the rotten egg that has harboured them. She sees it as clearly as Cassandra does.

Cassandra's cries rend the palace. Cassandra is sick with her crying; her whole body attempts to extrude what she has seen.

They hold her down; clean up the mess of mucus, vomit and faeces that spurts and dribbles out of her, but her large, shouted words drift away unheard. Helen alone recognises the truth of Cassandra's cries. But she says nothing, her perfect composure the exact opposite of Cassandra's disarray.

The egg is full of vipers. An endless supply of them: if you cut one two will form. They breed and breed.

Dark worms make their way up the hill like big fingers. Fat fingers thrumming on the sand; fingers walking, walking along the floor of her room, across its white walls.

Nearer they come. Nearer.

Her bed.

Her body.

Fat fingers walking. An endless supply. Cut one and two form. They breed and breed and nothing will stop them.

Not even the cries Cassandra hurls from the battlements as she crashes around the palace.

Helen is ten years old and has been building a little walled town out of twigs and mud. At the top of the largest building – she calls it her palace – she has stuck the russet feather of a pheasant. Tiny fragments of shell pave the streets and slivers of bark from plane trees make shingle roofs for the buildings. There is a temple in which she means to place a light if she can make or find one small enough. She wants there to be fire in her town. Water too. With a forefinger she has excavated a small well; she imagines it fed by the same streams as the great river she is digging out to flow at the side of the town. When she has finished scooping out the riverbed she fetches water in a jar and carefully pours some out. But she has not thought to line her riverbed and the water drains quickly away leaving only a muddy trace. She takes the jar again, tipping it by the handles she thinks of as its ears, filling her riverbed again with water. And for a few moments she has the satisfaction of seeing her river full to its banks and she wonders where she will construct a bridge for her townspeople to cross at. Then that water also drains away leaving a deeper paste of mud than before. Well then, it's summer, she thinks. The river has dried up. There is always water in the well if you let your bucket down far enough. She needs to make a bucket and some waterpots. An acorn cup and some small sea shells from her treasure chest.

She is thinking now of who will live in her town. She goes to the place in the wall where there is a gap and, making her first two fingers into legs, walks up the street to the palace. Then the first two fingers of her other hand walk up the street – or rather they run, in a hurry to join the first person at the palace with its feather flag flying. There's going to be a party.

When the man comes in – she has not invited him into the hut where she plays – he asks her about her game. It is not a game, she explains, but a town and this is the river that runs near it and it is summer so it has run dry. And this is the palace where visitors are arriving.

'Like me,' he says. 'Like me coming here to visit you in your palace.'

And with his great fat fingers he makes his way up the town street. When he gets to the palace door Helen is afraid he will push his way in. His fingers are too big and clumsy for the delicate frame she has made.

But he stops in front of the door.

This time Theseus stops.

From her high room in the palace Helen watches the men streaming up the hill. She feels each footfall as a print on her flesh.

The fat fingers keep walking till they come upon her and fasten. They push, tease, slide their way in where they should not go till her body feels like a cooking pot coming to boil; gobbets of meat rising and hurtling in different directions. Hot, muddled, excited, angry. The smell of meat's juices. The fingers stick to her so closely it's as if she has grown them; as if it's her own secret will doing this painful, confusing, exciting thing. If she, this slender ten-year-old child, could use her wrestling skills to throw him off and kill him she would do it, but he has her pinned down. She tries to cry out to her brothers but the fingers clamp down on her mouth. As he pushes in tighter and breaks her she knows that the smell on his fingers is partly her own.

~

THE MASSACRE begins in silence.

To each home in Troy, a Greek soldier. He enters by stealth like a burglar, jemmying open the locks; or he slides himself in through a window like a cat. He stands before a door, still, gathering the poise and purpose of a diver on the edge of a high dive. Then he kicks the door down with a sudden release of force. He eases himself, belly down, across a roof until he finds a weak point to dismantle – make a hole large enough for his body to drop through.

Throughout the city the throats of sleepers are cut.

Then the dogs start up their rumpus.

Mothers who run out into the street with their babies are met by dark-clothed soldiers with knives and clubs and ropes. Some attempt to hide their babies – in chests, in the jars where bread is stored, up chimneys. One tells her child to hide in the well she'd often forbidden him to climb down. There is a little shelf a short clamber down the well-shaft where he's crouched many times, hiding from friends. He stays there, shivering, listening to the dogs and the screams, seeing the bright gleam of the moon reflected in the water below him. After many hours the silver of moon-light is replaced by the gold of flame.

It is ten years since these Greek men have seen the families they left. Mothers and fathers have died in that time. Wives given birth to other men's children. Now they show what this has been like; the harm that's been done to them. Listen to the little sigh a child's body makes when you pierce it. See the mother's expression as you rape her with your hand, your penis, your spear, in the presence of her dead or dying child.

The palace is like another city; so many dwellings and quarters, linked by passages instead of streets, halls instead of market places. And while soldiers whose names we'll never know give vent to their injured lust and imagination to murder, loot, rape and torch the citizens of Troy whose names are also forgotten, the Greek commanders –

the celebrated warriors – do much the same amongst the palace's royal inhabitants. There are only so many parts you can slice or hack from a man or a woman; only so many holes and crevices you can fuck.

Of all the destroyers who move through the palace that day it is Neoptolemus who excels; who is the most unremitting. He makes his way through the rooms, eliminating life, thinking to emulate the father he's never met, whose armour he now wears. He wants someone to say, 'It's as if Achilles were living and moving again.' But not one person does.

Helen hears the cries of Hecuba, Cassandra, Andromache, Polyxena, the shrieks of the baby Astyanax, as if they were her own. The cries she has never been able to utter from that perfect, unfailingly beautiful mouth. And just as those cries are her cries, so the sheer, screaming, terrified chaos of the palace is hers also, as she sits composedly in her high room, waiting.

Flames from the town have already begun to lick the sides of the palace when Menelaus and his rout stumble, almost by accident, into the small room. They find her sitting, perfectly still, like a good little maid who has finished her job of hulling the strawberries and is now lost in reverie, bowl in lap, enjoying the sweetness of sun on her cheek. The others, drunk with the killing they've already accomplished, see only another object to destroy. It looks to Menelaus as if his own men will go for her.

'Leave us,' he says, barring their way with his spear.

The men brake themselves with difficulty.

Nothing in her appearance suggests the years that have gone by. Her skin is so soft you would imagine a breath might bruise it, let alone all those things her body has done and had done to it.

For a moment Menelaus is humbled by the wondrous thing that she is. Then a kind of glee begins to drift up through him in little bubbles; more and more of them, till he is fizzing with it.

'Mine,' he thinks. 'She's mine.'

He takes down one of the tapestries from the wall and wraps her in it to protect her from the flames.

In the well it grows hot. The flames that are romping through the city, eating it up, suck out the air from the well-shaft till there is none left to breathe.

And Neoptolemus – they call him Pyrrhus because of his hair – wipes his sword clean when he sees there is no one left to kill.

Vulnerary

When Chiron who made the ash spear gave it to Peleus on his wedding day he saw beyond Peleus to the son. And to the son's son and what he would do with it. He saw the blade gleam in the flames of the burning city.

Yet as he passed it to Peleus it was balanced so easily across his outstretched palms you might have thought it as light as a piece of cloth and not of a weight to make men stagger.

The tree which made it was always meaning to become a spear. He wonders now if there is a moment in the destiny of a tree when its future is open. When it is simply a quantity of wood – a material which may be used in a variety of ways to give shelter or fodder, adorn or destroy? Is he responsible for the outcome of what he made – did his seeing contribute to its destiny? For he never saw it as other than it became.

The tree began like any other – as a tiny, germinated sprout from a handful of green keys. Chiron had seen that the way above the shoot to the sky was unobstructed. He'd watched it grow and lopped back rival growth, keeping the vertical pathway clear so the tree was drawn up, as through a funnel, exceptionally tall and straight. The slender, central trunk divided into branches like burnished grey antlers, each nubbed with a sentient black bud, like a little hoof.

It had grown like a mast, pointing to heaven. But he knew it would not make a mast.

He sensed the ghost of the spear in the small sapling; saw the terrible bronze tip Hephaestus would make for it. It poked out through the leaves at the top of the tree, glinting in the sun.

It cut into the sky.

For twenty-two years he watched the ash tree grow and helped it on. When he saw it was ready he took an axe (whose handle he'd made from an ancestor of the tree) and felled it. He peeled the wood, seasoned it, planed it till it was perfectly smooth and taper. Tested the weight and balance. When Hephaestus delivered the spear-head, he fitted it; stepped back when Athene pushed in, insisting it was her job to finish it.

She blew a mist of breath on the shaft and buffed it with the edge of her shawl till it shone like polished bone.

~

To SAY that Chiron suffers is like saying that earth receives rain or that olive trees accept the winds which pummel and mould them till each is shaped like no other. Some people find a strip of seaweed which they hang at their window frame to catch the mood of the weather. By its puckerings and sweats they discover what they fail to read in the tissues of their flesh. The soft mouth of Chiron's wound catches every shift of wind: whether the air carries dryness, moisture, balm or ice. It catches each breath of animal pain and shares it.

This wound, received from Heracles, would have killed

any creature able to die. The arrow went in to his breast, just under the left foreleg, pressing in between ribs to lodge its tip in the smooth muscle of his large horse heart. Where it continues to bleed: a steady, agonising leak of blood which cannot kill him (the god-heart he carries in his man-trunk ensures this) and cannot ever be healed. It feels as if the arrow is still embedded. When he moves, walking or galloping, he has the sensation of it dangling from his chest, its shaft a little bit longer than the distance between chest and ground so it drags and catches, causing the point to stir in his heart and release more gusts of pain.

He has found no antidote to the poison the arrow was dipped in. Searching and intimate, it crawls and flashes around his body at all times.

The wound has become his laboratory.

In May the air on Pelion is sweet with the scent of apple blossom. Pelion's apples are the best in the world (no human there would choose a gold one). It is also the home of sweet and bitter herbs: demulcents, hepatics, astringents, analgesics, diuretics, emetics, expectorants, vulneraries, tonics and deadly poisons.

He has proved the effects of them all on his body. All the grated rhizomes, pappy stalks, crushed leaves and macerated seeds that he prepares he applies to his own wound. He feels how they affect the living tissue; how some contain enzymes which change its nature, eating it away, while others momentarily soothe and are balm to its rawness. But there are others yet that aggravate, making him wish he could tear off the caustic layer with his nails. There are times he could tear the heart from his horse's breast.

Years of experiment and practice made him a great and wise healer. But it is suffering – his own – which makes him the best. Because he can bear to suffer (though he cannot bear it, that is the trouble) he can judge exactly the extent of another's need and when it has been assuaged.

He knows who to treat, when to treat, and when to stop.

He knows that the smallest quantities are often the most effective.

He has taught (but only Asclepius has ever understood this) that the weapon which wounded you may sometimes be used to heal you.

The pain of others, far away on the plains of Troy, or the agony of a creature mangled in a trap: these nudge the phantom arrow tip and make his heart bleed.

He needed no visitor to tell him the war had begun. It was as if a herd of terrified cattle had crashed down off the edge of a precipice to land with all their hooves embedded in his breast.

AAAAIIIIIIIEEEEEEEE!!!!!

The hooves continue their lacerations for ten years. Sometimes it's a steady grinding; at other times a sharp and detailed agony makes him vomit and want to rear. If his body were less solidly planted, his nervous system less disciplined, he would dance wild with it, skittering crazy in the longing to cast it off.

But when Apollo's arrow pierces Achilles it is not pain he feels. For once there is no pain.

Instead, a sense of stopping. A silence, as if all the water-falls that spout and gush down Pelion's sides have ceased, their waters pooled somewhere else, somewhere still. As if life and colour have been sucked from the world. As if his own heart has suddenly emptied.

~

IT IS the curse of immortality to see those you care for die. (Even Zeus knows it, all those variously beloved mortal children – he cannot deify them all – snuffed out after a little breathing space.) Your children should be your immortality. Your pupils too. Chiron has seen too many of each grow up and die. Not all had the chance to grow old.

Which is worse? To watch the ardent child you've trained and nurtured grow dim-eyed, dried-out and faltering, while you, his father and teacher, remain unchanged – not young exactly, but unimpaired.

Or to see that child cut off before age has begun to eat his powers?

Either way, it feels wrong.

He climbs up onto a lip of rock that overhangs his high cave. From here he can see the Bay of Iolkos below him. Its wide, generous curve. Jason set out from here in the beautiful, fifty-oared ship – oars cut from the trees of this mountain. Two other foster sons – Peleus and Heracles – were part of that unparalleled crew. And Orpheus, who had the nerve to compete with the Sirens. He can remember the sound of the oars, dipping and lifting, dipping and lifting. The sound of the water as it streamed from the oars; the sight of the sun silvering the streaming water. Young men's voices singing in time with their raised oars. Youth, hope, confidence in vigour. All things sparkled: the sea, the oiled bodies, the eyes of the crew. And the far-away fleece which beckoned them with its scintillating impossibility.

So many have set out with high hearts.

He watched the Myrmidon fleet set sail for the muster at Aulis. Achilles, fresh home from Skiros to lead it.

When Thetis first brought him – wanting to see this famous foster-father with her own eyes before entrusting her son – the boy made Chiron think of a young fox: russet hair, quick, watchful eyes. The child Achilles liked to sleep curled up around the centaur's belly, cramming himself into the softness below the horse ribs. At these times Chiron felt himself a mother to the boy.

Yet the boy who took shelter in his body like an orphan was the bravest he'd ever reared. Quick too. Nothing stupid in his courage. Whatever Achilles did he did with the whole of himself. That was the power of it. If he stopped, he was still and the world fell upon his senses. When he moved, nothing restrained him. Other students were impatient of botany and biology in their longing to be heroes. The child Achilles loved the small life of the earth. He watched it, listened to it and applied himself to it. He who had little time or respect for the sons of Atreus honoured the kingdoms of termites and bees, was humble before the properties of plants.

Achillea: an excellent vulnerary which Achilles discovered. Chiron named it after him.

Now he feels old, tired, ridiculous. Still to be lugging this hoofed and hairy body around when so much of what he has cherished and shaped has gone. As if, without knowing it, Achilles had been his own quick heart out there.

Curiosity used to be enough. There is always more to know and more to find. More plants, more minerals, more processes, more ways of doing. More stars, and more to come.

(He cannot know that Zeus will one day make stars out of him: send Night crashing through his body, cleansing and purging it as no vulnerary could; punching his flesh through till all that is left is the pegs from which his frame once hung: the stars he becomes, aiming his bow for ever in the Southern Hemisphere.)

He would like more than anything to die in the ordinary way: lie down because his back and his limbs are tired, the walls of his vessels eroded with use.

He is not even a proper immortal. He cannot change shape. He obeys the mortals' laws of time and unfolding. Patience – hardly a divine attribute – is what he knows best and what he has attempted to teach. He is simply a mortal unable to die.

And so he goes on as before. Doing what he does as well as he can: learning, teaching, making, healing.

Interest – a tiny, unextinguishable flame – quickens again.

Each day as he goes through the forest he examines the

growing trees; sees what they may be:

A bow,

A spear,

A bowl,

A table,

A quiverful of arrows,

Sticks for his beans to climb up.

In spite of the wound he received from Heracles' arrow (an arrow made perfectly straight, perfectly fledged, just as he'd taught) he still makes bows and shows his pupils how.

What you need for a bow is wood, horn and sinew. Horn and sinew dress the skeleton of wood. You have to catch them, maybe using a bow made with parts of the creature's forebears. You will use the whole creature – eat the meat, cure the hide or the fleece, make glue from what's left. The glue you will use to attach the cut horn to the wood.

The more venturesome the animal, the tougher and better the sinew.

Once you have separated sinew from carcass you need to get rid of the fat and the bits of flesh that still adhere. Chiron scrapes these off with a blade and hangs what is left from a tree so birds can peck off the remaining fat.

You don't want to be handling greasy sinew.

Leave it to dry in the sun.

Now, take a wide mallet and beat the sinew, using a hard wooden block or a smooth rock as your anvil. Beat it until it has laid itself out in separate fibres, like coarse hair or the fibres of certain trees.

You can comb it, so the tangle of fibres lies orderly.

The best sinew for this job is the calcaneal tendon of any wild animal. Later called the Achilles.

Ash wood cleaves easily. It is both tough and elastic and has the capacity to absorb repeated shocks without communicating them to the handler's hand. Which makes it useful for oars, axe handles and bows. A good choice for a spear.

RELAY

Relay

'I feel more and more every day, as my imagination strengthens, that I do not live in this world alone but in a thousand worlds... According to my state of mind I am with Achilles shouting in the Trenches or with Theocritus in the Vales of Sicily.'

'I am afraid I shall pop off just when my mind is able to run alone.'

'Nothing is so bad as want of health – it makes one envy Scavengers and Cinder-sifters.'

'I cannot bear flashes of light and return into my glooms again.'

'every man who can row his boat and walk and talk seems a different being from myself – I do not feel in the world –'

'if I had had time I would have made myself remember'd.'

~

'PAY ATTENTION gentlemen', says Astley Cooper, 'I will show you. This specimen has been prepared already.'

The body lies on the table covered by a sheet, like a piece of best furniture to be protected from the sunlight.

Cooper nods to his assistant who obliges by turning back the top part of the sheet to reveal the grey and stubbled face of the dead man.

Keats leans forward. He doesn't want to miss a thing.

Cooper has taught that the physician should be possessed of the eye of an eagle, the hand of a lady and the heart of a lion.

He tips the head of the cadaver so that the chin touches the chest.

'Would you hold him thus,' he asks the dresser.

He proceeds to lift the upper portion of the skull as if it were a lid. Placing his fingertips at the rim of the cut skull he begins to draw the brain out; tenderly, as if he were easing a child into the world.

The man has been dead for some days. Cooper had the latest batch delivered to his home where he sometimes prepares his teaching specimens. It is autumn, no longer hot, so it will last a bit longer before the smell becomes unbearable.

The lifted brain sits on the table, the delicate skins of the arachnoid and the pia mater holding its shape. A grayish pink; pasty; coiled like a trellis. Or a rope of uncooked sausages.

Not as fluid as the brains of his father when they leaked out onto Finsbury Pavement.

'I could not have lifted the brain thus from the skull without careful preparation. I ask you to suggest why.'

A few answers are forthcoming.

'The dural membrane, sir. You have to cut it away, remove

the falciform and tentorial membranes from their attachment to the periosteal membrane lining the skull.'

'Quite right sir. Anything else?'

Someone suggests that nerves and blood vessels would have needed to be cut.

'Well done, well done. What else?'

Keats hesitates to speak. He has little confidence in his knowledge in this area but is prompted by an almost sympathetic sense of disturbance within his own brain.

'The hypophysis sir,' he mumbles. Then, ashamed of himself for lack of boldness, he recovers his lion heart and speaks out, 'The hypophysis. It sits in the *sella Turcica* – the Turkish saddle – of the *os sphenoidis* – you would need to sever the stalk before you could lift out the brain as you have done.'

'Very good,' says Cooper genially. 'Very good.'

He remembers the *os sphenoidis* from Bell's engravings. It reminded him of a giant butterfly with ragged, opulent wings. He touches his temples to feel the furthest reach of the wings that span his head. Feels – *Already with thee* – his own capacity for flight. The *sella Turcica* where the little bulb of the pituitary sits snug for its ride is well named. It also resembles an altar: a small table to bear a holy object.

At the centre of the brain, a sanctuary.

That night Keats dreams he is riding a pale stallion. He is galloping recklessly along a high ridge which overlooks a plain outside Troy.

He is seated securely in his fine Turkish saddle.

Like a saddle.

Like an altar.

(That euery like is not the same, O Caesar,
The heart of Brutus earnes to thinke vpon!)

The cold sac of coiled, dampish tissue was once a brain very like his own. In structure at least. His own warm hand – with which he writes, eats, ties his cravat, clasps other hands, pleasures himself etc. – is like the hand of him there, the cadaver whose right upper limb they'd seen displayed: nerve, muscle, tendon, bone. There are differences of course – variations in thicknesses, curves, placements – there was the man whose stomach had sagged right down into his pelvis. Differences in size. But even that great fellow who had gone to such lengths to ensure he wouldn't be made an anatomy of when they hung him – even his huge bones were of the same number, the same design, the same function as his own.

… the same and not the same.

'It is very unlike you my dear Keats to be so peevish.' How can I be unlike myself?

I was not myself at the time.

~

THEY SAID he must hurry down to the new picture gallery at Dulwich to see his likeness. Charles Cowden Clarke his old schoolmaster was the first to see it. Soon it was an established joke among his friends – 'Go to Dulwich to see Keats done by Rembrandt.' Keats went and looked.

It looked like a self-portrait though not, to him, a portrait of himself. Eyes facing directly ahead as they would to meet a mirrored gaze; nothing formal about the subject, though the auburn curls look newly washed and brushed (you can almost feel their softness). They lie like a fur collar against the russet jacket, giving it an air of richness. The jacket only a touch more red than the hair.

A study in reds.

The red of the jacket is picked up by the red of the parted lips. The subject seems to be breathing through them. The eyes are lustrous and dark (the same colour as the beret which stands as a smoky halo against the varying browns behind). The lines below them suggest tiredness and, perhaps, delicacy.

Hazlitt says, 'It is one of those portraits of which it is common to say "that it *must* be a likeness".'

Keats is conscious of not being tall. At one dismal gathering he heard someone say, 'O, he is quite the little Poet.' Insufferable. '*You see what it is to be under six foot and not a lord.*'

Severn observes that Keats is 'called up into grave manliness at the mention of anything oppressive'; seems 'like a tall man in a moment'.

Not a tall man. Like one.

'*I never feel more contemptible than when I am sitting by a good looking Coachman – One is nothing.*'

The only time Keats appears small is when he is reading.

The large Achilles (on his prest-bed lolling)
From his deepe Chest, laughes out a lowd applause

As Keats reads these lines he feels a little flood of satisfaction. He strokes them appreciatively with his thumb. The way the accents fall, on 'large', on 'prest-bed' – you can feel the weight of the man sinking into his bed, the words pressing, like the printer's ink, into the page. He takes his pencil to underline, to <u>double underline</u> this place. His chest eases, as if it were his own deep chest freeing itself.

'Ah,' he breathes in a low voice, 'that's nice.'

He triple scores the margin too, making this place, this book, his own.

~

MID SEPTEMBER. A day so balmy and sweet it would be a crime to stay indoors. Keats has been walking on the Heath for about an hour. Walking and composing go well together, the one rhythm feeding the other, imagination stretching and strengthening with his limbs. Often he sets out on a walk with a particular problem or sticking place in his mind and he thinks he will work on it as he goes. Then as he walks his mind empties and he becomes a window for what's around him, the problem he'd set out with forgotten.

This morning he has stopped walking to sit for a while on a hospitable hummock. Leaves are falling and he watches them: the way the air holds them as if reluctant to let them drop. A lock of hair hangs there too. Like another leaf, red-gold. And because the air itself is gold in this light, and warm and comfortable as exhaled breath, it falls slowly.

Keats watches it float and fall, fascinated by the way the sun catches the various strands and the way in which they are obviously separate yet still adhere together. By friction? Habit? Attraction? The lock, made of so many independent entities, has itself an identity.

He holds his hand out, waiting for the lock to fall onto it, which it gently does – unlike leaves which often elude him at the last minute. How nearly weightless it is. He can hardly feel it (though he could feel it if it moved – if a girl were to brush his cheek, his lips, with a little tuft of her own hair). He takes from a pocket a small book – a volume of Cary's Dante – slips it in between the leaves for safe-keeping.

He forgets about it until later that day when he takes out his Cary again and it falls open at the same place. It is the passage where Dante sees Achilles in Hell. In the second circle, with Paolo and Francesca. With the lovers.

Keats runs to Brown's desk and seizes a pair of scissors; tugs down a piece of hair from over his brow and cuts it. He places the two side by side. They appear exactly the same: the same deep auburn. The floating hair looked lighter in the sunlight as Keats' hair will sometimes flash gold in the sun.

. . . the same and not the same.

Whose head shed this? Whose vital force gave body and colour to this hair so like his own? Hunt surprised him the other day with a real authenticated lock of Milton's hair. Keats wrote an ode on it.

> *When I do speak, I'll think upon this hour,*
> *Because I feel my forehead hot and flush'd –*
> *Even at the simplest vassal of thy Power –*
> *A Lock of thy bright hair – sudden it came,*
> *And I was startled when I caught thy name*
> *Coupled so unaware –*
> *Yet at the moment, temperate was my blood –*
> *Methought I had beheld it from the flood –*

But whose power's vassal was this?

Someone taking advantage of the sunshine to get a little barbering done on the Heath.

'Our bodies every seven years are completely fresh-materiald ... We are like the relict garments of a Saint: the same and not the same: for the careful Monks patch it and patch it: till there's not a thread of the original garment left and still they show it for St. Anthony's shirt.'

He has thought about soul-making; but what about body-making? The cadavers he has seen (the resurrectionists always kept Astley Cooper well supplied) so clearly *relicts*. So clearly no longer men, or women. More like a kind of deposit. The leavings. The imprint left when the soul has gone. Like fossil traces of the soul.

Our bodies – not remade from scratch every seven years but constantly eroding and renewing until the renewal stops. What persists most is what is least alive. Scar tissue for example – intractable, durable stuff. Once the body has rallied to repair itself the site of repair becomes fixed; unable to renew itself any more.

The more durable, the less living.

The more solid, the less real.

'I will clamber through the Clouds and exist.'

It takes energy, some kind of ardent pursuit, to exist, to be distinct, to be real.

'I go among the Fields and catch a glimpse of a stoat or a fieldmouse peeping out of the withered grass – the creature hath a purpose and its eyes are bright with it – I go among the buildings of a city and I see a Man hurrying along – to what?

The Creature has a purpose and his eyes are bright with it.'

The look of a creature, fully alive. It is this that Hazlitt saw in the Dulwich portrait. It may make a man resemble a horse, a bird, an otter, a stoat.

'What a set of little people we live amongst. I went the other day into an ironmonger's shop, without any change in my sensations – men and tin kettles are much the same in these days.'

ANTONY: *To the Boy Caesar send this*
    grizled head, and he will fill thy wishes to the brimme
    With Principalities.
CLEOPATRA: *That head, my lord?*

The head she has cradled, caressed; whose lips, tongue, mouth have aroused her, answered her. How can that ever be a thing to send?

This living hand, now warm and capable / Of earnest grasping ... will one day, possibly soon, be part of the earth: interred. It will become waterlogged, and the small life of the earth will begin to take it apart. It is unpleasant to think that the nails and the hair will continue to grow for some time: their life independent of any controlling consciousness.

> *Who hath not loiter'd in a green church-yard,*
>   *And let his spirit, like a demon mole,*
> *Work through the clayey soil and gravel hard,*
>   *To see scull, coffin'd bones, and funeral stole;*
> *Pitying each form that hungry Death hath marr'd,*
> *And filling it once more with human soul?*

This living hand, the relict garment of a saint.

'*it was not this hand that clench'd itself against Hammond*'
nor this same hand that last clasped yours.

But there is a connection.

The most intimate continuity between cell and cell. The
part that's born has touched the part that dies and the dying
body is parent to the living.

Like a relay. The baton passed from hand to hand.

Or like a chain of fire. The beacons proclaiming that Troy
has fallen – the news carried from high point to high point,
swift almost as thought, till it reaches the heart of Achaea
and the remotest islands; till Clytemnestra knows, and
Penelope, and Peleus.

If continuity between cell and cell, between my hand now
and my hand then, so also between man and man. This
hand that clasped your hand that clasped his hand and so
on. As if the warmth in my veins were passed back to run in
his who lived so long ago.

My father, me thinkes I see my father.

Is it the same song – though sung by another nightingale –
that I hear now as Ruth heard, sick for home? Different
lungs and larynxes to be sure. Different ears too. But is there
enough the same?

A game of Chinese whispers. A hot word thrown into
the next lap before it burns. It has not been allowed to set.
Each hand that momentarily holds it, weighs it, before
depositing it with a neighbour also, inadvertently, moulds
it; communicates its own heat.

From cheep to chirp.
From woof to warp.

'We read fine things but never feel them to the full until we have gone the same steps as the Author.'

Who are we when we read? Or when we really listen to the story of another? When we *attend* a performance? Is there not a tiny, palpable, nervous participation: the thin end of a wedge whose wide end is visible action? Do we not, in a small way, imitate?

CORIOLANUS: *... I will not doo't,*
  Least I surcease to honor mine owne truth
  And by my Bodies action teach my Minde
  A most inherent Basenesse.

We are what we do.

One of the things which we do is imagine.

' ... even now I am perhaps not speaking from myself; but from some character in whose soul I now live.'

～

' ... THE FIRE is at its last click – I am sitting with my back to it with one foot rather askew upon the rug and the other with the heel a little elevated from the carpet... These are trifles – but I require nothing so much of you as that you will give me a like description of yourselves... Could I see the same thing done of any great Man long since dead it would be a great delight: As to know in what position Shakespeare sat when he began "To be or not to be" – such things become interesting from a distance of time or place.'

～

THE RELICTS of a saint are not moved by those acquisitive of their virtues. They are *translated*: carried across. A chain of hands across the waters, across the mountains, across time, conveying the precious changed and changing thing.

('*Yet through all this I see his splendour ... I am ... straining at particles of light in the midst of a great darkness.*')

Chapman's Homer. The *Iliads* written in fourteeners (Keats uses the metre for a walking poem): in it appear angels; whales.

There Keats reads of Patroclus' funeral:

They rais'd a huge pile, and to arms went every Myrmidon,
Charg'd by Achilles; chariots and horse were harnessed,
Fighters and charioters got up, and they the sad march led,
A cloud of infinite foot behind. In midst of all was borne
Patroclus' person by his peers. On him were all heads shorn,
Even till they cover'd him with curls. Next to him marcht
*   his friend*
Embracing his cold neck all sad, since now he was to send
His dearest to his endless home. Arriv'd all where the wood
Was heap'd up for the funeral. Apart Achilles stood,
And when enough wood was heapt on, he cut his golden
*   hair*
Long kept for Spercheus the flood, in hope of safe repair
To Phthia by that river's power;

Peleus had vowed in vain that Achilles' long hair would be offered to the river on his safe return from Troy. Achilles speaks:

> '. . . since I never more
> Shall see my lov'd soil, my friend's hands shall to the
> Stygian shore
> Convey these tresses.' Thus he put in his friend's hands the
> hair.

Keats remembers the lock that landed on him that day on the Heath and tugs again at his hair. He would like to shear some off this time in honour of Achilles and place it in his hands. To pave his own way to the Stygian shore. And, though he cannot place it in Achilles' hands, he cuts his hair anyway, enjoying the crunch of the scissors on it, realising that Achilles would have used a knife or the edge of his sword. He holds in his own quite delicate hand a hank of auburn hair, not yet made dull or lank by illness. The same colour as Achilles' hair and, though the hand which holds it may be smaller than that of the large Achilles, it is made in the same way, the same number of small bones. It holds and releases its contents in a similar way, using similar muscles ('*Thus* he put . . .'). It is prompted by similar nerves. Fed by a like heart.

It gives him great pleasure to know this.

GLOSSARY OF
CLASSICAL NAMES

ACHAEA Greece.

ACHERON One of the rivers of Hell.

ACHILLES Son of King Peleus and the sea nymph Thetis; Prince and commander of the Myrmidons; the Greeks' greatest warrior.

AGAMEMNON Son of Atreus, king of Mycenae and Commander in Chief of the Greek army; brother of Menelaus and husband of Clytemnestra.

AJAX A mighty Greek warrior; son of Telamon and leader of the troops from Salamis.

ALCIMUS A Myrmidon commander.

AMAZONS A race of women warriors, fighting as allies of Troy.

ANDROMACHE Wife of Hector and mother of Astyanax.

ANTIELUS A Greek; one of those in the wooden horse.

APOLLO Son of Zeus and Leto, brother of Artemis; associated with music, archery and healing. This god supports the Trojan cause.

ARTEMIS Daughter of Zeus and Leto, sister of Apollo; associated with hunting, chastity and fertility.

ASCLEPIUS A great healer, educated by Chiron; father of Machaon who inherits his skills.

ASTYANAX Son of Hector and Andromache; killed in infancy by Neoptolemus at the Sack of Troy.

ATHENE Daughter of Zeus (from whose head she was born, fully armed); defender of the Greeks.

ATLAS Once a Titan, now a mountain that supports the heavens.

ATREUS Son of Pelops; father of Agamemnon and Menelaus.

AULIS Harbour on the narrow strait between Euboia and the Greek mainland where the Achaean fleet gathers and from where it sets sail.

AUTOMEDON Charioteer to Achilles and Patroclus; Achilles' best friend after Patroclus.

BRISEIS A war-prize of Achilles and loved by him.

CASSANDRA Daughter of Priam and Hecuba, a princess of Troy. Apollo – with whom she mated – gave her the uneasy gift of accurate prophecy which would never be believed.

CASTOR Brother of Helen and Polydeuces.

CHIRON The wise centaur who educated Peleus, Achilles and many other heroes.

CIRCE A sorceress living on the island of Aeaea; Odysseus interrupts his journey home from the war to be her lover for a year.

CLYTEMNESTRA Wife of Agamemnon whom she murders on his return from the war.

DEIDAMIA Daughter of King Lycomedes of Skiros; Achilles' first female lover and mother of Neoptolemus.

DEIPHOEBUS Son of Priam and Hecuba; younger brother of Hector.

DIOMEDES One of the Greeks' finest warriors.

ELEPHENOR A Greek commander.

EUMELOS A Greek commander; one of those in the wooden horse.

EURYDAMAS A Greek commander; one of those in the wooden horse.

EURYPLOS A Greek; one of those in the wooden horse.

FURY An avenging spirit. The Furies are traditionally female.

HECTOR Son of Priam and Hecuba, husband to Andromache, father of Astyanax. He is Troy's greatest hero.

HECUBA   Queen of Troy; wife of Priam.

HELEN   Daughter of Zeus and Leda; wife of Menelaus. Her abduction to Troy by Paris is the cause of the war.

HEPHAESTUS   God of fire; chief artificer among the gods.

HERACLES   Greek hero, renowned for his Labours; educated by Chiron whom he inadvertently wounds with a poisoned arrow.

HERMES   A son of Zeus; a god of quick wits and changing shapes.

IDAEUS   Priam's herald. His name ('from Mount Ida') is common among Trojans.

IDOMENEUS   Commander of the Cretan fleet.

IOLKOS   City near Mount Pelion on the Greek mainland. The Argonauts set sail from the Bay of Iolkos.

IPHIGENEIA   Daughter of Clytemnestra and Agamemnon; sacrificed to Artemis at Aulis in obedience to an oracle stating that the Greek fleet would be becalmed until this happened.

IRIS   A goddess; Zeus' messenger.

ITHAKA   The island home of Odysseus.

JASON   Commander of the Argonauts; educated by Chiron.

JUNO   Queen of the heavens; wife (and sister) of Zeus.

LAERTES   King of Ithaka and father of Odysseus.

LEONEUS   A Greek; one of those in the wooden horse.

LYCOMEDES   King of Skiros; father of Deidamia.

MACHAON   Son of Asclepius; a Greek commander and valued healer.

MEGES   A Greek commander; among those in the wooden horse.

MENELAUS   King of Lacedaemon, brother of Agamemnon and husband of Helen. The Greeks' second in command.

MERIONES A Greek; Idomeneus' second in command; one of those in the wooden horse.

MNEMOSYNE Mother, by Zeus, of the nine Muses; her meaning is Memory.

MUSES Goddesses of the arts; daughters of Zeus and Mnemosyne. There are nine of them: Clio, Euterpe, Thalia, Melpomene, Terpsichore, Erato, Polyhymnia, Calliope and Urania.

MYRMIDONS The people of Phthia ruled by Peleus. They are said to have originated as ants.

NEOPTOLEMUS Son of Achilles and Deidamia. He is also known as Pyrrhus (red-head).

NESTOR King of Pylos; the oldest and wisest of the Greek chiefs.

NIOBE A woman of Phrygia whose twelve children were killed by Apollo and Artemis.

ODYSSEUS Son of Laertes, king of Ithaka, and husband of Penelope. The most strategic of the Greek leaders.

OLYMPUS The highest mountain on the Greek mainland; the gods live at its summit.

ORPHEUS A Thracian musician and singer of extraordinary power; one of the Argonauts.

PARIS A Trojan prince, son of Priam and Hecuba. His abduction of Helen is the cause of the Trojan war.

PATROCLUS Achilles' cousin and best beloved.

PEDASUS The mortal horse among Achilles' team of three.

PELEUS King of the Myrmidons; father of Achilles.

PELION A mountain in Magnesia on the Greek mainland; home of Chiron the centaur.

PENELOPE Wife of Odysseus.

PENTHISELEIA Queen and Commander in Chief of the Amazons.

PHAEDRA Wife of Theseus whose passionate, unmet love for her step-son Hippolytus led to his death and her suicide.

PHEIDIPPOS A Greek; one of those in the wooden horse.

PHILOCTETES A Greek commander whose snake-bitten foot stinks so much that his fellows abandon him on the island of Lemnos till the need for Heracles' bow (which Philoctetes has and without which Troy will not fall) leads Odysseus to send Neoptolemus to fetch it and, in the event, Philoctetes.

PHOENIX A Greek; deputed by Peleus to act as father-figure and tutor to Achilles during the Trojan expedition.

PHTHIA On the Greek mainland, to the east of Mount Othrys; home of King Peleus and birthplace of Achilles.

POLYDEUCES Brother of Helen and Castor.

POLYXENA Daughter of Priam and Hecuba.

POSEIDON God of earthquakes and the sea; a brother of Zeus.

PRIAM King of Troy, husband of Hecuba.

PYRRHA The name that Achilles assumes when he is disguised as a girl at Skiros.

SCAMANDER The chief river of the Trojan plain.

SIRENS Sea nymphs whose irresistibly charming song leads sailors to shipwreck.

SKIROS The island to which Thetis takes Achilles disguised as a girl.

SPARTA On the southern Greek mainland; home of Helen and Menelaus.

SPERCHEUS A swift-flowing river in Thessaly.

STYX One of the rivers of Hell.

THESEUS King of Athens.

THETIS A sea nymph; mother of Achilles.

TIRESIAS   An infallible prophet who has lived as both man and woman.

TROY   The capital of Troas; a walled city near Mount Ida on the north-west coast of Asia Minor; ruled by King Priam and at war with Greece since the abduction of Helen by Priam's son Paris.

ZEUS   King of the gods.